Jack Higgins

Writing as Harry Patterson

DILLINGER

Pan Books
London, Sydney and Auckland

First published by Hutchinson 1983

This edition published 1989 by Pan Books Ltd,
Cavaye Place, London SW10 9PG

9 8 7 6 5 4 3

© Harry Patterson 1983

ISBN 0 330 30714 2

Printed and bound in Great Britain by
Richard Clay Ltd, Bungay, Suffolk

Dillinger is derived and expanded from the
author's earlier novel *Thunder at Noon*, which was
originally published in 1964 by John Long

For Geoff and Irene
– not forgetting Sarah,
Kate and Rebecca

INTRODUCTION

Early in March 1934, John Dillinger, the most notorious
criminal in American history, made a spectacular escape
from Lake County Jail, Crown Point, Indiana. What happened to him in the period following his escape has always
been a matter of speculation. He was reported to have
been seen in Chicago, New Orleans, California, New
York, even in London. And there were those, of course,
who insisted that he was safe over the border in Mexico.
Perhaps it went something like this . . .

I

Dillinger lay on his bunk in one corner of the cell, his head pillowed on a hand, staring up at the ceiling. His cell mate in the 'escape-proof' new section of Lake County's three-storey brick jail, Herbert Youngblood, a big Negro, stood at the window gazing out through the bars down into the street in front of the jail.

Dillinger said, 'What's it like out there?'

'Must be two, maybe three hundred people,' Youngblood said. 'Hell, it's worse than the State Fair. They got National Guard out there in uniform, like they were going to war.' He turned, smiling. 'Maybe they think you're planning on taking a trip?'

'It's a thought,' Dillinger said calmly.

There was the rattle of a key in the lock of the sliding cell door, a row of vertical bars. They turned to see an old man wearing faded denims, holding a tray, Sam Cahoon, the attendant.

'Coffee, Mr Dillinger?'

'Why not?'

Dillinger sat up and the old man placed two tin cups on the small table and filled them, the pot shaking a little in his hand so that he spilled some.

'You been across to the hotel this morning?' Dillinger asked as Cahoon passed him his coffee.

'I sure have, Mr Dillinger,' Cahoon said. 'They're sleeping on the floors. More folks coming in all the time.

They've got reporters, radio people, a newsreel cameraman. You should get a commission from the hotel, Mr Dillinger.'

He smiled in a strained, anxious way as if conscious that he might have gone too far. Dillinger sipped his coffee thoughtfully and it was Youngblood who answered for him.

'A great idea, Pops. Next time you're over there, you tell the guy who runs the joint Mr Dillinger was asking about his cut.'

'I sure will,' Cahoon said eagerly. 'More coffee, Mr Dillinger?'

'No thanks, Sam. This is just fine,' Dillinger told him.

The old man picked up the tray. On the other side of the bars was one of the trusties with a mop stuck in a bucket.

'I was told to bring this here,' the trustie said.

Cahoon slid the bars to the side just enough to let the man squeeze by and put the bucket and mop down next to where Dillinger was sitting. Quickly Youngblood said, 'I'll do that.'

The trustie, who looked very nervous, said, 'I was told to give it to Mr Dillinger.' He scurried out, followed by Sam, who locked the sliding bars behind him.

'Idiots,' Youngblood said. 'What good's a mop and bucket without water?'

Dillinger held a finger up to his lips. He went over to the bars and checked right and left, then with his back to the bars in case anyone came along unexpectedly, he squatted down and carefully lifted the mop end from the bottom of the bucket and took out something wrapped in flannel.

'Stand next to me,' he whispered to Youngblood.

Their backs a screen in case anyone approached, Dillinger unwrapped the flannel. In its centre was a blue-black .32 calibre Colt automatic. Quickly, Dillinger checked the clip, saw that it had all eight rounds, and jammed it back into the handle.

'Let's have your knife,' Dillinger said.

Youngblood produced a bone-handled pocket knife from the top of his right boot and handed it across. Dillinger sprung the blade, instinctively tested it on his thumb, and told Youngblood, 'Stand by the bars. Anyone comes, you tell me fast.'

As Youngblood leaned backwards against the bars, Dillinger reached under the mattress on his bunk, slit it, and shoved the Colt into the slit. He tested to see if it was far enough away from the cut not to fall out accidentally. Only then did Dillinger look up at Youngblood with a smile.

There was amazement in Youngblood's eyes. 'Jesus, Mr Dillinger,' was all he said.

The lounge of the hotel was crowded, reporters three deep at the bar, and the noise made it necessary to shout to be heard. The young woman, sitting alone at the bamboo table by the window where she could view the street, looked out of place in the neat two-piece black suit and cream oyster-satin blouse, her blonde hair framed by a close-fitting black velvet hat.

The man who approached her, glass in hand, was perhaps thirty-five, with a world-weary, sardonic face. A grey fedora was pushed to the back of his head.

'Hello,' he said. 'Mike Jarvis, AP. I hear you're with the Denver Press.'

'That's right, Martha Ryan.'

'Can I get you a drink?'

She lifted her cup. 'Coffee's just fine, thank you.'

He sat down and offered her a cigarette. 'They sent you up here to get the woman's angle, I suppose?'

'That's right. Only it doesn't look as if anyone's getting in to see him' she shrugged.

11

'Well, there's the sheriff,' Jarvis said, nodding toward the large window.

'Oh, where is he?' Martha Ryan said, standing.

Jarvis laughed. 'He's a she,' he said, pointing to where a middle-aged woman flanked by two male deputies was crossing the street. 'Her husband was the sheriff of Lake County. When he got himself killed, she took over for the rest of his term, like they did in the olden days.'

The door opened and Lillian Holley entered and was immediately surrounded by excited newsmen, all talking at once. The two brawny deputies started to push a way through the crowd for her and she called in exasperation, 'Can't a girl get a cup of coffee in peace round here.'

Jarvis, watching her speculatively, turned suddenly to Martha Ryan. 'She won't let any one of the guys see Dillinger at the moment, but what if I persuaded her to let you in?'

Martha Ryan stared at him sceptically. 'You think there's a chance?'

'Maybe, only one thing. You share your story with me and no one else. Is it a deal?'

She reached across and pressed his hand. 'A deal, Mr Jarvis.'

He stood up as Lillian Holley pressed forward. 'Hey, Lillian! Over here!'

She paused, glancing towards him. 'Mike Jarvis, you still here? You don't give up, do you?'

Her eyes considered the young woman and she came forward and Jarvis held his seat for her. 'Here, take this.'

She sat down and the two deputies stood guard, backs towards her, arms folded, and the crowd of reporters retreated to the bar.

'Introduce me, Mike,' she said.

'Miss Martha Ryan of the Denver Press.'

Mrs Holley frowned. 'Your editor must be crazy, ex-

12

pecting a kid like you to hold her own with a bunch of villains like these guys. Just out of college?'

'That's right, Mrs Holley.'

A waiter appeared with fresh coffee. Lillian Holley said, 'I get it, he wants a fresh angle. Why thousands of red-blooded American women have the hots for Johnny Dillinger.'

Martha Ryan blushed and Jarvis said, 'It's the little lady's first big assignment, Lillian.'

'Next thing, you'll be telling me her ageing mother's in the hospital and she needs the money.'

Jarvis grinned and turned to Martha. 'Hey, you didn't tell me.'

Martha Ryan smiled. 'I won't lie to you, Mrs Holley. Any kind of story from here would get me a byline and could make my career.'

Lillian Holley looked her over calmly. 'Well,' she said, 'it's nice to see a woman ambitious for a change, instead of all these hustling men.'

Martha Ryan said, 'Just five minutes with him? Please Mrs Holley, it could be my break.'

Jarvis patted Martha Ryan's hand. 'Too much to expect, angel. I mean all these guys here have been hanging around for days trying to see John Dillinger. They'd go crazy. No, it can't be done.'

Lillian Holley noticed how Martha Ryan gently moved her hand away from Jarvis's condescending pat. 'You men,' she said to Jarvis, taking his bait, 'think you know everything. Who the hell do you think is in charge around here? If I say this girl sees Dillinger, she sees him and there's nothing those creeps can do about it.'

'Sorry, Lillian, no offence meant,' Jarvis said hastily.

Lillian Holley leaned across the table to Martha Ryan. 'I'll give you five minutes, that's all, you understand?'

The girl stared at her in amazement. 'You mean it? You really mean it? Five minutes with Dillinger.'

'Hey, you got a great title for your feature there,' Jarvis told her.

Lillian Holley said, 'I'm leaving now. Give me a couple of minutes, then report to the back entrance of the jail. You'll be expected. And keep it to yourself for now.'

'Oh, I will, Mrs Holley,' Martha Ryan said.

Lillian Holley stood up and turned to Jarvis. 'And that goes for you, too. Keep your mouth shut on this one, Mike, or don't come back.'

She nodded to the two deputies and followed them to the door.

Martha Ryan said, 'I can't believe it.' She turned to Jarvis as he sat down again. 'Have you any idea what this could mean to me, Mr Jarvis?'

'Sure I do,' he said. 'New York, next stop.' He lit another cigarette. 'And what I said about sharing the story. Forget it. This one's yours. Who knows, maybe you could get a Pulitzer.'

She was almost in tears. 'But why are you doing this for me? I don't understand?'

'Simple,' he said. 'I work out of AP's New York office myself. Maybe if you get there, you'll let me buy you a cup of coffee some time.' He smiled, reached across to pat her hand.

Instead, Martha Ryan took his hand and pumped it. 'Thank you, Mr Jarvis,' she said.

'Call me Mike.'

'Thank you, Mike.'

Jarvis smiled. 'Now get the hell out of here and get your story.'

Youngblood, leaning against the door, watching, now made a quick gesture. 'Someone's coming.'

Dillinger quickly lay on the bed. As he lit a cigarette the key rattled in the lock, the sliding bars opened and a guard

14

stood to one side as Lillian Holley entered followed by the young woman.

'On your feet, Johnny,' Mrs Holley said. 'I'd like you to meet a lady. This is Miss Martha Ryan of the Denver Press and I've told her she can have five minutes with you.'

'Hell, Mrs Holley,' Youngblood said, 'I could do with five minutes there myself.

As Youngblood spoke, there was the most extraordinary change in Dillinger. He was on his feet in an instant, his face pale, his eyes very dark so that Youngblood recoiled as from a blow in the face.

'Sorry, Mr Dillinger,' he whispered.

Dillinger turned to Martha Ryan, his charming half smile on view again. 'Miss Ryan, what can I do for you?'

She was, for a moment, almost overcome. He was not what she thought he'd be. Though he was shorter than she'd expected, his shoulders were those of a bigger man. His restless, intelligent face and pleasant, courteous voice carried a curious authority.

Her throat was dry, but she managed to speak. 'Well, I know your background, Mr Dillinger, everyone does. Your family, that kind of stuff. I just wanted to ask you some other kinds of questions.'

He pulled a chair forward. 'Fire away.'

She took a pad and pencil from her purse. 'They say you intend to escape from here. Is that true?'

The question was so naive that Lillian Holley laughed harshly and answered it for him. 'This section of the jail, honey, the new section, is escape-proof. That's the way the architect designed it. Even if he got through that door he'd have to pass through God knows how many gates and armed guards.'

Dillinger turned to the girl. 'Satisfied?'

'But they say your friends are coming to get you out.'

15

'What friends? If I had friends, they wouldn't be stupid enough to try to crash Mrs Holley's Indiana Alcatraz, would they?'

The half smile was still firmly in place, as if he was laughing at the world and everyone in it. 'However, if an attractive honey like you'd come along for the ride, I might decide to try for the outside.' He winked at Mrs Holley. 'Course, Mrs Holley could come along as chaperone.'

Martha Ryan wasn't sure whether he was making a pass or a joke or both at the same time. She tried again. 'Have you any interest in politics, Mr Dillinger?'

'Not until Mr Roosevelt came along. You can say I'm for him all the way, and for the NRA – particularly for banking, only he'll have to hurry.'

She looked genuinely bewildered. 'I don't understand, you're a . . .' She hesitated.

'A thief?' He said helpfully. 'True. I rob the banks, if that's what you mean, but who do they rob, Miss Ryan? Indiana, Kansas, Iowa, Texas – take your choice. People thrown off their farms wholesale while the banks foreclose, then sell out at a huge profit to the big wheat combines.'

'Business, Johnny,' Lillian Holley said dryly. 'Just business.'

'Oh, sure, the kind that makes me feel clean,' Dillinger said. 'Six millions unemployed out there, Miss Ryan. You ask them what kind of a thief John Dillinger is.'

She sat there staring up at him. He didn't sound that much different from some of the editorial writers she'd met. Lillian Holley said, 'OK, angel, that's it,' and pulled her up, a hand under her elbow.

Martha Ryan held out her hand. 'Thank you, Mr Dillinger and good . . .' She swallowed the words, blushing.

Dillinger laughed. 'I wouldn't put that in your article if I were you. They mightn't understand.' And then he smiled gently. 'Don't worry about me, Miss Ryan. I know the

16

road I'm taking, I know what's at the end of it. My choice! No one else's.'

Martha recoiled instinctively. Dillinger's courtly smile had changed into a stone mask. She went out, wanting to glance back, Lillian Holley followed. The door closed behind them. Dillinger stood there for a moment, then felt inside the mattress and took out the pistol.

'Are you with me?' he asked Youngblood.

'You crashing out, Mr Dillinger?'

'That's it.'

'The guy I killed was trying to stick a knife in me, but I could still get the chair, Mr Dillinger, him being white. That don't leave me much choice, so I'm with you.'

'Good, when the time comes just do as I say and I'll get you out of here,' Dillinger told him.

He took his jacket out of the cupboard, put it on and slipped the pistol into his right-hand pocket, then he lay on the bed and closed his eyes, thinking of his father. Boy that old son-of-a-bitch would be surprised if his bad boy walked in the door.

As one of the deputies unlocked the door at the rear of the prison, Lillian Holley said, 'Well, what did you make of him?'

Martha Ryan was bewildered and showed it. 'I expected a monster, not a . . . ladies' man.'

'I know. It's very confusing. You know there are people who argue that he's never even killed anybody.'

'I can't believe that.'

'I'll tell you one thing. He's an Indiana farm boy, born and bred, and wherever he travels in the back country, people know, but they don't turn him in, not for any reward. Can you explain that to me?'

'No.'

'Well, when you can, you'll have your real story.'

She shook hands and Martha Ryan passed outside and the door closed behind her.

When Cahoon unlocked the door of Dillinger's cell he was carrying a bucket full of soapy water which he put down by the wall.

'OK, Herbert,' he said to Youngblood. 'Cleaning time.' He straightened and found himself staring into the muzzle of a Colt automatic, steady in Dillinger's hand. 'Jesus Christ,' he said softly.

Dillinger got off the bed. 'Just do as I say, Sam, and we'll get along. Understand?'

'Anything you say, Mr Dillinger,' Cahoon told him eagerly.

'Who's out there?'

'The cleaning detail, all trusties. They won't give you no trouble.'

'Any guards?'

'No.'

'What about down in the old jail?'

'I saw Deputy Sheriff Blunk down there a few moments ago.'

'Fine, we'll get to him in a second.'

Dillinger moved out into the long corridor, cells opening off it. There were about twelve men out there, all trusted prisoners as Cahoon had said, the cleaning detail starting the day's work, talking cheerfully amongst themselves.

Dillinger moved closer and paused. The man nearest to him saw him almost at once and stopped in the act of squeezing out his mop in the bucket, an expression of astonishment on his face. His stillness passed through the others like a wave. There was silence.

'Everyone inside.'

Dillinger motioned with the pistol and stood back as they filed past him into the cell. There was no trouble, but with men like these, he didn't expect any.

18

He said to Youngblood. 'You stay here. I'll be back.'
He nodded to Cahoon. 'Let's go.'

When Deputy Sheriff Ernest Blunk on duty on the first
floor heard Cahoon call to him, he went up the stairs
without hesitation to find Dillinger waiting for him, gun
in hand.

'Oh, my God,' Blunk said, more frightened than he had
ever been in his life before.

Dillinger relieved him of the pistol he carried on his
right hip and slipped the gun into his pocket. 'Is anyone
else down there on your landing?'

Blunk, a prudent man, saw no reason to argue. 'Nobody, Mr Dillinger.'

'And the warden?'

'Mr Baker's in his office on the ground floor.'

'OK, then we go down and get him.' He pushed Cahoon
along the corridor towards Youngblood who was standing
outside the locked door of their cell, holding the key. 'Put
him in with the others and wait here.'

As Blunk had said, the corridor below was deserted and
they moved along it and paused at the top of the stairs
leading to the ground floor.

Dillinger said, 'Go on, you know what to do.'

Blunk sighed and called, 'Hey, Lou, you're wanted up
here.'

'What the hell for?' a voice called back and Warden
Lou Baker appeared at the bottom of the stairs and started
up briskly. He was almost at the top when he looked up
and saw Dillinger standing there, gun in hand.

He stopped dead in his tracks and in the circumstances
stayed surprisingly cool.

'Johnny, what in the hell do you think you're playing
at? You ain't going anywhere. You got at least ten National Guardsmen at the front entrance armed with machine guns.'

19

'Well, that should make things interesting,' Dillinger said calmly. 'Now upstairs, both of you.'

A few moments later and Youngblood was putting the Warden and Blunk in the cell with the others. He locked the door. 'OK, what happens now?'

'Stay here,' Dillinger told him. I'll be back.'

Youngblood said, 'You wouldn't leave me, Mr Dillinger?'

'The most important thing you should know about me,' Dillinger said. 'I never ran out on anyone in my whole life,' and he turned and moved away along the corridor.

The man on duty that morning at the barred gate which gave access to the jail offices at the front of the building was a trustie, who was sitting at his desk, reading a newspaper. The headline said: 'Public Enemy Number One Finally Caged'. There was a photo of Dillinger to go with it. A slight tapping sound caused the trustie to look up and he saw the man himself peering through the bars just above him, a gun in his hand.

Dillinger said softly, 'Open up!'

The trustie almost dropped his keys in his eagerness to comply, but, a moment later, had the gate open. The office door stood partly ajar and someone was whistling in there.

'Who is it?' Dillinger inquired softly.

'National Guardsman.'

'Just the one?' The man nodded and Dillinger said, 'Call him out.'

The trustie did as he was told and a second later the door opened and a young National Guardsman in uniform appeared. There was instant horror in his eyes and he got his hands up fast.

Behind him on the table were two loaded Thompson sub-machine guns. Dillinger moved past him and stared down at them for a monent. 'Well, I'll be damned,' he said. 'Thank you.'

He slipped the pistol into his other pocket, picked up a machine gun in each hand and turned to the two men. 'OK, now we're going to go upstairs, all the way up to the top landing in the new wing. You fellas see any problems in that?'

'No, Mr Dillinger,' they assured him eagerly and the trustie turned and led the way.

A few minutes later, Youngblood, clutching one of the machine guns, was shepherding them into the cell on the top landing with the others. Dillinger said, 'Let's have Blunk out here again.'

Youngblood pulled the deputy sheriff out and closed and locked the door. 'Now what?' he demanded.

'We're clear, all the way down to the jail office and the front entrance, only that's too public by far.'

'So what do we do?'

'Walk right out of the back door and this is the man who's going to show us the way, isn't that so, Mr Blunk?'

Ernest Blunk sighed heavily yet again. 'If you say so, Mr Dillinger.'

'Oh, but I do,' Dillinger said. 'In fact, I insist,' and he pushed him along the corridor.

It was raining when they emerged from the door at the rear of the prison ten minutes later and moved along the alley. Dillinger and Youngblood wore raincoats taken from three local farmers they had found eating in the kitchen. The farmers were now locked in a washroom.

'The garage?' Dillinger said to Blunk. 'How far?'

'Right down there a hundred and fifty yards,' the deputy told him.

'OK,' Dillinger said. 'You lead the way and just remember what I'm holding under this raincoat if you feel like calling out.'

He raised the machine gun slightly, the muzzle poking through, and Blunk said hastily, 'No trouble, Mr Dillinger, not from me. We got this far, haven't we? All I want is to see you off my hands.'

He led the way, following a route which took them past the Criminal Courts building and, a few moments later, entered the side door of a large garage. There was a single mechanic in oil-stained overalls working on his own.

He glanced up. 'Hello there, Mr Blunk.'

It was apparent that he didn't recognize Dillinger and Blunk said, 'Ed Saager, the best mechanic in town, Mr Dillinger.'

Saager looked shocked and Dillinger produced the machine gun from under his raincoat. 'Which car here's in the best shape?'

'Why, that would be the Ford here,' Saager told him. 'Mrs Holley's car.'

'Engine tuned?'

'Like a watch.'

'Fan belt OK?'

'Replaced last month.'

'Pick-up?'

'Best in the lot.'

'Then that's what we'll take. You get in the rear with my friend and you, Mr Blunk, can take the wheel.'

Saager opened his mouth as if to protest, thought better of it and got into the rear seat with Youngblood. Blunk took the wheel and started the motor as Dillinger got in beside him.

'Nice and easy, Mr Blunk,' he said as they turned into the main street. 'No need to hurry.'

He leaned back and lit a cigarette calmly.

Mike Jarvis and Martha Ryan were sitting in a booth at the rear of the hotel lounge enjoying a late breakfast when there was a sudden excited murmur and a voice called, 'Dillinger's escaped.'

Jarvis jumped to his feet and moved out and Martha

Ryan sat there, suddenly cold, aware of the excited hub-bub of voices outside.

Jarvis came back a moment later and sat down. 'My God, would you believe it. That place was supposed to be escape-proof. Not only did he walk right out, he's used the sheriff's car for his getaway.' He threw back his head and laughed. 'Jesus, will Lillian be mad.'

But Martha Ryan simply sat there, the coldness growing within her, aware only of Dillinger's final words to her. That he knew the road he was taking. That he knew what lay at the end of it.

It was still raining and they were over the border into Illinois when Blunk, on Dillinger's orders, pulled up at the side of the dirt road they had been following.

'OK,' Dillinger said. 'This is where you two get off.'

They got out of the car reluctantly, uncertain as to his intentions, but Dillinger just drove away, the wheels of the big Ford churning mud, and Dillinger hoping some of it would land on Blunk's suit.

Youngblood started to sing loudly in the rear seat. A few miles further on, Dillinger stopped the car to light a cigarette, then he took a few crumpled bills from his pocket and counted them.

'Fourteen dollars isn't going to get us very far.'

'And that's a fact,' Youngblood said. 'I guess there's only one thing to do. You'll just have to rob a bank, Mr Dillinger.'

He started to laugh and Dillinger, loving the feel of being behind the wheel of a fast-moving car, feeling as exhilarated as a kid, tossed him the cigarette pack and drove away through the rain, wondering what the newspaper headlines would be saying in the morning.

2

Doc Floyd came up out of the hollow and followed the overgrown path through the trees, pausing at the edge of the swamp to light his pipe. He was seventy years of age, with a worn and wrinkled face, the grey moustache stained with nicotine. His straw hat was frayed at the edges and the old alpaca coat hung from bony shoulders.

The garden on the other side of the track was overgrown, the fences broken and the clapboard farmhouse beyond was dilapidated, shingles missing in places from the roof. There was an atmosphere of decay to everything.

An old hound dog nosed out of the undergrowth and limped towards him and Doc Floyd leaned down and fondled its ears.

'All wore out, Sam, just like you.'

He straightened at the sound of a car approaching and said softly, 'Looks like they're here, Sam. Let's go.' and he went up through the broken fence towards the house, the dog trailing him.

When he went round to the front, a de Soto sedan was parked there. The man in the dark suit who leaned against it, wiping sweat from his face, fanning himself with his hat at the same time, was middle-aged and overweight. His name was George Harvey and he was manager of the Huntsville National Bank. The man beside him could have been any one of a hundred local farmers to judge by his faded jeans and sweat-stained felt hat. The only difference

24

was the deputy's badge on his chest and the pistol in the holster on his left hip.

Harvey said, 'Ah, there you are Doc. You know Larry Schultz?'

'Sure I do,' Doc said. 'Mary OK now, Larry? I heard she was under the weather.'

'It was nothing. She's fine now.' Schultz was embarrassed and it showed.

'OK, let's get down to business,' Harvey said. 'The bank's been very patient, Doc, but enough is enough. I have to ask you formally now. Are you in a position to settle?'

'You know damn well I'm not,' Doc told him flatly.

Harvey turned to Schultz. 'Serve your papers.'

Schultz produced a folded document from his shirt pocket and held it out to the old man who took it from him. 'Sorry Doc,' he said.

Doc shrugged. 'Not your fault, Larry, we all got to eat.'

Harvey got behind the wheel of the de Soto and switched on the motor. 'OK, Larry, let's go. I'm a busy man.'

Schultz went round to the other side and got into the passenger seat. Doc ran a finger over the gleaming paintwork. 'Some car, Mr Harvey. I suppose a car like this must cost a heap of money?'

'Seven days, that's what you've got,' Harvey said. 'Then the bank forecloses and that means everything, Doc, so don't you move a damn thing out of here.'

He drove away very fast, spraying dirt, and disappeared along the track through the trees towards the main road. Doc Floyd stood there for a long moment, then turned and mounted the steps to the porch and went inside, the dog following him.

He found a half-full bottle of whisky and a glass and sat at the table in the untidy, shabby room, drinking slowly, savouring it as if it might be the last drink he was likely to have.

His eyes roamed around the room, taking in the sagging furniture, the worn carpet, and finally came to rest on the photo of his wife in the old silver frame.

'Not much to show for forty years of living, old girl,' he said softly.

He toasted her, emptied the glass in a quick swallow and poured another.

It was perhaps an hour later that he became aware of the sound of a car approaching up the track outside and by then he was drunk enough to be angry.

'The bastard, Sam,' he said softly to the dog. 'Back already.'

He stood up, took an old double-barrelled shotgun down from the wall, found some cartridges in a drawer, and loaded it as he went to the door. The hound dog whined anxiously and followed.

Doc stood on the porch outside, the gun ready in his hand, only the car which had stopped in the middle of the yard wasn't the de Soto. It was a Ford coupé and the man in the black felt hat and neat dark suit who slid out from behind the wheel was definitely not George Harvey.

'Hello, Doc,' he called softly. 'That's a hell of a welcome.'

Doc lowered the shotgun in astonishment. 'Jesus Christ,' he said. 'Johnny Dillinger. You shouldn't be here. They come looking for you just day before yesterday.'

'Who's they?'

'A bunch of lawmen. Come in two cars. Fellow who asked about you stutters. Tall, wiry, big fellow.'

Dillinger laughed. 'That must be Matt Leach. He runs the Indiana State Police.'

'I wouldn't laugh, Johnny. He said he'd break my ass

if I was lying to him about your being here. He said he'd break your ass when he caught you.'

'Somebody sent him a dime book called *How To Be a Detective*', Dillinger said. 'He thinks it was me.'

'Was it you, Johnny?'

Dillinger rolled his eyes like Al Jolson. A picture of innocence.

'Oh you're a terrible man, Johnny.'

Somewhere thunder rumbled and there was that sudden quiet moment before a storm when everything seemed poised for a terrible downpour.

Dillinger said, 'Mind if I come in? I think it's going to rain.'

'Sure, sure, Johnny, but what if Leach comes back,'

'I'll just bring my insurance policy into the house with me if you don't mind.' Dillinger went back to the Ford. Doc watched him bring in the machine guns as if death was being carried into the house under both of Johnny's arms.

And then the rains came, a heavy relentless downpour that churned the yard to mud as Dillinger sat on the porch, drinking Doc's coffee and cleaning his tommy guns to perfection. The old man's plaint was getting to him, making his eyelid tic.

'Three thousand lousy bucks by next Monday,' Doc was saying, 'or they take over – even the furniture.'

'Can't you sell some of your land off and settle up your debt to the bank?' Dillinger asked.

'Not possible,' Doc said. 'Not under the terms of the mortgage. And there isn't enough time That bastard George Harvey is collecting as many small farms as he can and hoarding them for resale when times get better.'

The old man poured another drink. 'Anyway, enough about me. What about you? That break from Lake View prison the other month must have been really something, wasn't it, Johnny?'

'For them, not for me,' Dillinger said. 'It was a breeze.'

'You're really number one, Johnny,' Doc said. 'I've known them all one time or t'other. None like you. I heard you was in California. The radio said you robbed a bank in Los Angeles last week.'

'Sure wish I did. I heard I was in Houston and New Orleans doing the same thing on the same day. It's OK with me. Just keeps the cops confused. What about your wife, Doc, she leave you on account of your drinking, the way she always swore she would?'

'She left me all right, Johnny. Died last year. Top of that, my girl Carrie, who married a guy from Miami, well he got himself killed asleep at the wheel last year, and Carrie took the baby with her to the Florida Keys. She runs a café down there.'

'Why don't you join her?'

'I couldn't do that to her. I'd just be a burden. A dried-up old man with no money.'

Dillinger said, 'I remember when this was the best hide-out in Kansas. A man could get anything here. A night's sleep, a change of car.'

Doc chuckled. 'Remember the night I took that bullet out of your arm after the Fort Harris job?'

Dillinger smiled faintly. 'You were a pretty damn good doctor for a country vet.'

'Oh, I had my moments.' He poured another whisky. 'It's funny, Johnny, but when you reach my age, you get to thinking what it's all supposed to be about.'

'Any answers?'

'Oh, sure – three thousand dollars, that's what my whole life adds up to, only I ain't got it which means my life adds up to nothing. That's a hell of a thing to contemplate.'

Dillinger sat there staring at him for a moment, then he stood up, picked up the old man's yellow oilskin slicker, pulled it on and went down the steps to the Ford.

'Where you going in the rain, you damn fool?' Doc yelled after him.

When Dillinger came back, he was carrying a small case which he carried inside and placed on the table. He opened it carefully. Inside, there was a stack of money, each bundle neatly banded in a bank wrapper.

The old man's eyes widened.

'Fifteen grand there, all I have to show for a misspent life,' Dillinger smiled. 'Keep it for me. If I don't come back, use it any way you see fit.'

'No, Johnny, I couldn't,' Doc whispered. 'God, where are you going?' the old man demanded.

'To see a man about a bank loan,' Dillinger said, his back to the old man as he went down the steps to the Ford, got behind the wheel, and drove away.

George Harvey glanced at his watch. It was just after 2.30 and it occurred to him that an early finish might make sense today. The relentless rain which had cleared the streets of Huntsville outside hammered ceaselessly against the window of his office and filled him with acute depression. He was about to get up, when the door opened and Marion, his secretary, looked in.

'Someone to see you.'

Harvey showed his irritation. 'I don't have any appointments.'

'No, he knows that. A Mr Jackson of the Chicago and District Land Company. Says he's only in town by chance and wonders if you could spare him a few minutes.'

'Does he look like money?'

'I'd say so.'

'OK. Bring him in, give it five minutes and then come in to remind me I've got another appointment.'

She went out and returned a moment later to usher Dillinger in. He held the yellow slicker over one arm and Marion took it from him.

29

'I'll hang it up for you.'

'That's very kind of you.'

She felt an unaccountable thrill as she went out, closing the door behind her, and Dillinger turned to face Harvey.

'It's good of you to see me, Mr Harvey.'

Harvey took in the excellent suit, the conservative tie, the soft-collared shirt in the very latest style, and got to his feet.

'That's what we're here for, Mr Jackson. Take a seat and tell me what I can do for you. You're in the property business?'

'That's right. Chicago District Land Company. We're in the market for farm properties in this area – suitable farm properties. Our clients, the people we represent in this instance, intend to farm in a much more modern way. To make that pay, they need lots of acreage. Know what I mean?'

'Exactly,' Harvey said, opened a box on his desk and offered him a cigar. 'I think you'll find you've come to the right place, Mr Jackson.'

'Good.' Dillinger took the cigar and leaned forward for a light. Harvey frowned. 'You know, I could swear I've met you some place before.'

'That could be,' Dillinger said. 'I get around. But let's get down to business. I need a bank down here.'

'No problem.'

'Good, then I'd like to make a withdrawal now.'

'A withdrawal?' Harvey looked bewildered. 'I don't understand.'

'Yes,' Dillinger said. 'Twelve thousand dollars should do it, what with my expenses and all.'

'But, Mr Jackson, you can't make a withdrawal when you haven't put anything in yet,' Harvey explained patiently.

'Oh, yes I can.' Dillinger took a Colt .45 automatic from his pocket and placed it on the table between them.

30

Harvey's whole face sagged. 'Oh, God,' he whispered. He looked at the man's face and it came to him. 'You're John Dillinger.'

'Pleased to meet you,' Dillinger said. 'Now we've got that over with, you get twelve grand in here fast and then you and me will take a little ride together.'

Dillinger walked over very close to Harvey so that the banker could feel Dillinger's breath on him.

Harvey was not a religious man. He went to church on Sundays because his customers went to church. But he found himself hoping that his Maker was looking down right now to protect him.

'Are you going to kill me?' Harvey asked.

'You're going to kill yourself, Mr Harvey, if you keep shaking that way.'

They both heard the door open. Quickly, Dillinger pulled his gun arm in and turned so that it wouldn't be seen from the door. It was Harvey's secretary, saying, 'Your next appointment is here, Mr Harvey.'

There was a slight pause. Dillinger waited and Harvey took a deep breath. 'Cancel it. They'll have to come in tomorrow, and tell Mr Powell I want twelve thousand dollars in here.' He glanced at Dillinger. 'Will fifties be OK?'

'Just fine,' Dillinger said amiably.

The woman went out. Dillinger put the Colt in his right-hand pocket, stood up and walked round the desk behind Harvey. 'You got a briefcase handy?'

'Yes,' Harvey said hoarsely.

'When he comes, put the money in that. Then we leave.'

The door opened a moment later and the chief cashier, Sam Powell, entered, carrying a cash tray on which the money was stacked. 'You did say twelve thousand, Mr Harvey?'

'That's right, Sam, just leave it on the desk. I'll clear it tomorrow.' He improvised fast. 'I'm into a situation that requires instant cash.'

'Too good an opportunity to miss,' Dillinger put in.

Powell withdrew and Harvey took his briefcase from under the desk, emptied it and started to stack the cash inside. He looked up. 'Now what?'

'Get your coat,' Dillinger said patiently. 'It's raining outside or hadn't you noticed? We walk right out the front door and cross the street to the Ford coupé.

'You're going to shoot me?' Harvey said urgently.

'Only if you make me. If you behave yourself, I'll drop you outside town. You can have a nice long walk back in the rain to think about it all.'

Harvey got his coat from the washroom and put it on, then he picked up the briefcase and moved to the door. 'Now smile,' Dillinger said. 'Look happy. Here, I'll tell you something funny. You know what guys in your position always say to guys like me in the movies? They say, "You'll never get away with it." '

And Harvey, nerves stretched as tight as they would go, started to laugh helplessly, was still laughing when they went out to Marion's office and picked up Dillinger's oilskin slicker and felt hat.

Sitting at the table, the screen door open, Doc Floyd heard the car drive up outside. He straightened, glass in hand, the other on Dillinger's case and waited fearfully. Dillinger appeared in the doorway, the briefcase in one hand. The dog whined and moved to his side and he reached down to scratch its ears.

He tossed the briefcase on to the table. 'Three thousand in there plus a little interest. Twelve thousand in all. That seem fair to you, Doc?'

The old man placed a hand on the briefcase and whispered, 'You kill anyone, Johnny?'

'No. I found your friend Harvey a real cooperative

fellow. Left him ten miles out of town on a dirt road to walk back in the rain.' He unfolded the paper from around a stick of chewing gum. 'You can pay what you owe on this dump now, Doc, or take the money and run all the way down to the Florida Keys and that daughter of yours.' Dillinger popped the gum into his mouth. 'Want some?'

'What about you, Johnny? That fellow Leach . . .'

'To hell with him.'

Doc wrung his hands. Just then they both heard the car in the distance.

'That coming this way?' Dillinger asked.

'Any car you hear ain't on the main road. Get in the back room, Johnny, quick. Take the briefcase. Take the guns. Anything else around here yours?'

Doc turned clear around, spied the coffee cups, put them in the sink. The only thing he saw in the room that frightened him was the look that came into Dillinger's eyes.

'Please go into the back room. If you shoot it out with someone here, win or lose, I'll never get to see my grandchild in Florida, Johnny. Please?'

Dillinger went into the back room, taking the briefcase and guns. As soon as he slammed the door, Doc rushed out of the house. Thank heaven, the rain had stopped, he thought. He wanted to meet the car as far from the house as he could.

He could see it was a Model A, black as they all were, spewing a cloud of mud behind it. The man driving didn't look familiar. Then Doc saw that a woman was sitting beside him.

The man turned the engine off and got out. 'Evening,' he said.

Doc nodded. He'd seen traps before, man and woman in the front, three men hiding behind the seat.

The man said, 'Me and the Mrs kind of got lost.'

'Where you headed?'

'Moline.'

33

'You got a long ways to go.'

'Know that. We figured to stop in a hotel some place tonight. Or thought maybe we could pay someone to stay over.'

'You don't want to stay here,' Doc said. 'My woman has black fever.'

The man didn't know what black fever was any more than Doc did, but he took a step backward.

'I can get you some water,' Doc said.

'No, thanks,' the man said. 'We'll be shoving off. When I get to the road, I turn left or right?'

'Left's the only way that'll head you toward Moline. There's a town an hour down the road got rooms above the general store.'

'Thank you kindly. You want us to tell the sheriff or anybody to send a doctor for your wife?'

'I'm a doctor.'

The man got back into his car. He didn't believe Doc was a doctor any more than he believed in the man in the moon.

'She's dying,' Doc said, 'and we want to be left alone for what time's left.'

'I appreciate that,' the man said, got in the car, and drove off slowly so as not to scatter too much mud in Doc's direction. Doc hurried to the house, opened the door of the back room, said, 'It's OK, Johnny. Travellers. Sent them on their way.'

'I hate this.'

'Hate what, Johnny?'

'Hiding like a rat. I wasn't made for it. I want to walk around like a free man.'

'You'll sure be able to do that,' Doc said, 'soon's the heat's off. Johnny, I'm old enough to be your father. You been real good to me so I'm going to chance saying something.' He wished Dillinger wasn't looking at him with those stony eyes.

'Say it!'

That man was sure on edge, Doc thought. 'You take too many chances. You've got to head south, I don't mean Texas, I mean all the way to Mexico, where they can't catch you, Johnny.'

'That means getting across the border.'

Doc poured whisky into a spare glass and pushed it across to him. 'Listen, Johnny, a few years back I had dealings with a guy who ran people into the country from Mexico illegally. European refugees, people like that.'

'So?'

'West of El Paso, there's a small town called Sutter's Well. Used to be a silver mine. It's a ghost town now. The back trail out of that town crosses the Mexican border. No border post, no customs, no police. That's the way we used to bring them in.'

'Will it take a car?'

'Oh, sure. Dirt road, but sound enough. You need to carry plenty of spare gas. Six or seven five-gallon cans in the trunk should cover you. Couple of spare fan belts. I can let you have a set of tools. Know your way around an engine, Johnny?'

'I know my way around a car, Doc, the way a cowboy knows his horse.'

'Good. I can give you the address of a Mexican in El Paso, big fat fellow called Charlie, can get you a passport that looks better than the real thing, just to cover you in case you get picked up.'

'I'm not planning to get picked up.'

'I know you're not planning to get a bullet hole in your radiator either, Johnny, but be damn careful.'

'That Ford out there is going to be hotter than hell when Harvey gets back to town. I'll need to switch cars.'

'I can help you there,' Doc said eagerly. 'You take me down to the south barn in the woods. I'll surprise you.

Here, better take your twelve thousand back. And take your hardware. You might need both in Mexico.'

He carried the case for Dillinger, who carried the machine guns. They went out, got into the Ford, and Dillinger drove round to the rear of the farm and followed the track down through the trees beside the swamp, following the old man's directions, finally braking to a halt beside an old dilapidated barn in the trees.

They got out and Doc unbarred the double doors, Dillinger helping him and pulled them back. A white Chevrolet convertible stood there. It looked brand new.

'And where in the hell did you get that?' Dillinger wanted to know.

'Kid called in here about six months ago named Leo Fettamen. You heard of him?'

'I don't think so.'

'Strictly small stuff, but as car crazy as you claim to be, Johnny. Fettaman robbed a bank in Carlsberg. Bought this and an old Ford with the cash. Went into Huntsville in the Ford with a guy who called himself Gruber. They intended to take the bank, come back here and use the Chevvy as their getaway car. The kid had a theory that the more imposing you looked, the less the cops were likely to stop you.'

'What happened?'

'Killed in a gun battle with the sheriff and his deputies. Hell, I think half the town put a bullet in them before they were finished. The righteous are terrible in their wrath, Johnny.'

'So I've noticed,' Dillinger said.

'Obviously I couldn't start riding around in it. That would have caused talk. Seeing's you got eyes for it, Johnny, I'll make a deal with you. It's yours for twelve thousand dollars.'

Dillinger smiled and slapped his hand. 'Doggone, you got it.'

'One thing you'll need from that Ford is the battery. The one in the Chevvy couldn't be flatter.'

Dillinger drove the Ford into the barn beside the Chevrolet, then got a wrench from the tool kit and removed the battery. It was only five minutes' work to substitute it for the battery in the other car, then he slid behind the wheel, pulled the choke and applied the starter. The Chevrolet's engine started instantly, purred like music.

As he got out, the old man was already transferring his belongings from the Ford. 'Anything I've forgotten?'

'You could say that.'

Dillinger lifted the rear seat of the Ford, revealing a shot-gun and two automatic pistols.

'You going to war, Johnny?' Doc asked.

They stowed the shotgun and pistols along with the rest of the arsenal under the rear seat of the Chevrolet. 'That's it,' Dillinger said.

The old man shook his head. 'No, the Ford, Johnny. That's got to go.' He nodded across the track to the swamp. 'In there.' He slapped the car on the roof with the flat of his hand. 'Seems like a waste, but when a man gets too greedy, he can end up on the end of a rope.'

Dillinger reached in and released the handbrake, then went round to the rear, and they got their shoulders down and pushed. The Ford bounced across the track, gathered momentum and ran away from them down the slope, plunging into the dark waters below. They stood there watching it disappear, Dillinger lighting a cigarette and offering the old man one. Doc shook his head and put his empty pipe in his mouth, chewing on it until the roof of the Ford had disappeared under the surface.

'That's it.'

They went back to the barn and got into the Chevrolet, and Dillinger drove back to the farm, braking to a halt at the foot of the porch steps. He started to open his door and Doc shook his head.

'You've got to get moving, Johnny. Let's cut it now.'

'Whatever you say, Doc.' Dillinger held out his hand.

Doc said, 'I want you to know I'm going to take your advice. I'm going south to the Florida Keys with money in my pants and it's all thanks to you.' He got out of the car and closed the door, leaning down to the window. 'I'm going to get some warmth into my old bones before I die and that's thanks to you as well, Johnny.'

Dillinger smiled. 'Good luck, Doc.'

He drove away through the rain and the old man stood there listening to the Chevrolet's sweet sound fade into the distance. Then he trudged across the muddy yard to the barn and opened the doors. An old Ford truck stood inside. He started it with the handle and drove it across to the front of the farm and went inside.

When he reappeared, he was carrying a suitcase and the briefcase, no more. He put them into the cab and went back up the steps into the living room. The hound dog moved restlessly beside him. It was very quiet, only the rain humming on the roof.

'Quiet, Sam,' he said gently. 'We're leaving now.'

He took out his pipe, filled it methodically from his worn tobacco pouch. Then he picked up the photo of his wife in the silver frame and slipped it into his pocket.

He struck a match on the side of his shoe and put it to the bowl of his pipe, then took the cowl of the oil lamp on the table and touched the match to the wick. It flared up and he reached forward and very gently turned it on its side. It rolled, coal oil spilling across the table and dripping to the floor, tongues of flame leaping up.

'Why, damn me, Sam,' Doc said to the hound. 'We appear to have a fire on our hands. Time to leave, I'd say.'

He went out and down the steps, holding open the door so that the old dog could climb up on the passenger seat. He went round to the front, swung the crank, then got behind the wheel and moved into gear. As he drove away, he started to sing softly:

'John Dillinger was the man for me,
He robbed the Glendale train,
Took from the banks, gave to the poor,
Shan't see his like again.'

Behind him, flames burst through the shingle roof and black smoke billowed into the air. Doc hadn't been happier in years. Then he remembered the man who'd come calling, Leach. The son-of-a-bitch had the whole of the Indiana State Police to catch one man. He hoped Johnny would be across the state line by now. Or real soon.

In his Washington office, J. Edgar Hoover had seven grown men standing around his desk as if they were page boys instead of high-ranking G-men. Hoover's voice was calm, but the men who had worked with him knew that he was furious.

'He phoned me,' Hoover said.

Of course they knew already. It was the scuttlebutt of headquarters.

'He phoned me collect. He said I should tell the President not to close any more banks.'

The men standing there kept straight faces because they knew what Hoover's fury would be like if they so much as smiled.

'He's made more headlines than movie stars. I don't want the kids in this country growing up emulating that man. Understand?'

They all nodded.

'The local boobs can't catch him, and when they do, they can't hold onto him. I want John Dillinger taken by the Bureau. Dead or alive.'

It was the man standing next to Purvis from Chicago who said, 'Any preference?'

Hoover laughed so they all thought it was OK to laugh too.

Hoover stood up for the first time. 'Here's my plan.'

3

In Texas he'd driven with the top of the white convertible down, hoping the breeze would help. Maybe not feeling safe yet was adding to his discomfort. But once he was across the border he felt safe, and the hot sun seemed to bear down on him even more, and he finally pulled over to the side of the dusty road, and raised the top to keep the sun off his head. He put the turned down panama hat beside him on the seat to let the sweat band dry out a bit, damn glad he'd bought it and thrown the straw hat away. He didn't want to look like an American from a mile away.

With his fingertips he felt the moustache he'd started to grow on the ride down. He glanced in the rear-view mirror. It was coming in black. All he needed was a better suntan.

Above the town the Sierras floated in a purple haze. He bet it was cooler up there, but he had to find a decent hotel, if there was such a place. Across the Plaza Civica that fronted the church, he saw it: the Hotel Balcon, a squat pink building with a crumbling façade. It had been used as a strongpoint during the revolution and the walls were pitted with bullet holes.

He pulled the white Chevrolet up in front of it, aware of the eyes watching him from the park. Maybe from windows up there too. Should he have stuck to a black car like most other people drove, not a white convertible that called attention to himself? He loved the goddamn car and didn't care about anything except that it was now covered in dust and grime. These people sure had lousy roads compared to the States.

Dillinger put on his linen jacket, took the one suitcase. Everything else was safely stowed in the trunk.

He noticed but didn't pay any attention to the older man who sat on the bench in front of the hotel, smoking the stub of a cigarette the way people who can't afford cigarettes did, dragging smoke out of the last half inch.

As Dillinger passed, the man said, 'Hi.'

Dillinger stopped. He certainly didn't recognize the old fellow in the crumpled linen suit. He had the face of a man who'd lived hard all his life. A grizzled beard framed his wide mouth.

Dillinger'd been worried about knowing only a few phrases in Spanish and here was this guy saying, 'Hi.' Then, 'Can you spare two bits?'

Dillinger put his suitcase down. 'How'd you know I spoke English?'

'You walk like an American. And I never saw anybody down here drive a job like that.' He pointed at the convertible. 'Besides,' he said with a small-time laugh, 'Illinois plates don't grow on cars down here. Two bits and I'll watch your fancy job while you check in.'

'What's it need watching for?'

'The kids around here'll be down on it three seconds after you walk in that front door. I'm cleaned out. Two bits and nobody gets near your car.'

Dillinger took out his wallet and extracted a five dollar bill. 'Watch it real good.'

The man examined the bill, his face lit up as if he'd just won a jackpot. 'Thank *you*,' he said, stretching the 'you' out.

Dillinger picked up his suitcase again when he heard the

man say, 'Don't I know you from somewhere, mister? You been in Laredo?'

'No.'

'San Antone?'

'No,' Dillinger said, and headed up the steps to the hotel entrance.

'Hey, I know who you look like,' the old man said. 'You look like John Dillinger.'

Dillinger looked around to see if anyone was standing within earshot. The only person close enough to have heard was a fat Mexican woman carrying a basket on her head. No chance she'd know the name even if she'd heard.

'I seen your picture,' the man said. 'You're him, ain't you?'

Dillinger turned slowly and moved back to face him. 'You're mistaken, friend. The name's Jordan – Harry Jordan.' He parted his jacket slightly so the old man could see the butt of the Colt pistol holstered under his left arm. 'You should be more careful, old timer. Americans should stick together in a place like this.'

The old man said, 'I guess I made a mistake. I'm sorry.'

'Make them myself every day,' Dillinger said and went into the hotel.

On the balcony above the hotel entrance, sitting well back out of the sun, the man who'd rented the best room in the hotel had listened to the exchange with interest. Although he hadn't heard the actual words, the new *gringo* spoke with an authority he liked. He picked up his Malacca cane, and straightening his wide-brimmed hat, he headed down to the lobby, walking with the confident gait of a man who knew what he wanted.

Dillinger, waiting at the desk for his key, saw him coming in the mirror. He was tall, with good shoulders, his temples brushed with grey, and the broken nose looked out of place in the aquiline face. There was an elegance about him, a touch of the *hidalgo* in the way he carried himself. He was a breed the revolution had almost destroyed. The proud ones who never gave in. Who had to be broken.

He removed the long cigarillo from his mouth. 'Senor Jordan?' he inquired in careful, clipped English.

Dillinger froze. How did the man know the name on his passport? No point in denying it. The hotel clerk knew. The old man in front knew. 'Yes,' was all Dillinger said.

'Allow me to introduce myself. Don Jose Manuel de Rivera.'

Dillinger could tell from the way the hotel clerk nodded to the man that he was a wheel.

'My business can be stated quite briefly, senor,' Rivera said. 'Perhaps I could accompany you to your room? We could talk as you unpack.'

'We can talk right here in the lobby,' Dillinger said, gesturing to a glass-topped wicker table with two chairs beside it.

'As you wish,' the man called Rivera said.

Just then they both heard the commotion outside, and a cracked voice yelling, 'Scram! Vamoose! Get the hell out of here!'

'Excuse me,' Dillinger said, and walked quickly to the front entrance, where, as he suspected, the old man was trying to chase away three shirtless teenage Mexican boys, one of whom had already opened the near door of the convertible and was peering into the glove compartment.

With quick strides Dillinger was at the car and grabbed the kid by his hair and yanked him out of the car, then twisted the kid's arm behind his back, paying no attention to the stream of Spanish invective. Calmly, Dillinger looked at the other two boys, who were standing on the running board on the other side. Whatever they saw in his eyes, plus the yelping of their friend, sent them dashing down the street.

The old American came around so he could yell at the captive's face. '*Ladron! Ladron!*'

'What the hell does that mean?' Dillinger asked.

'Thief.'

'Tell him I'm going to break his arm so he won't steal any more.'

The old man translated it into rough Spanish. The kid looked frightened.

Then, with one motion, Dillinger flung the kid to the ground, giving him a chance to scamper away.

Dillinger laughed, and only then did he notice that the whole scene had been observed by Senor Rivera from the doorway.

'Bravo, Senor Jordan,' Rivera said.

'I apologize for the intermission,' Dillinger said, 'but I really like that car the way it is.'

'Understandable.'

The old man, his face a mask of disgrace, was holding out the five dollar bill Dillinger had given him. 'I guess you want this back. I didn't do too good watching your car for you.'

'You did fine. If you hadn't yelled, I wouldn't have come out. Just what I wanted.' He reached under the front seat of the car and pulled out a big flannel rag. 'Here. Why don't you clean the dust off the car while I talk to this gentleman. If you're dusting it, I don't think anybody else will bother it.'

'Absolutely, Mr Jordan,' the old man said, taking the rag and hastily pocketing the five-dollar bill again.

Rivera said, 'Perhaps now we can talk in your room where it will be quieter, senor?'

Dillinger hesitated and then shrugged. 'Why not?'

He collected his suitcase from the front desk and led the way up the broad wooden stairs to the first floor and unlocked the door at the end of the corridor. The room was like an oven. The fan in the ceiling was not moving.

45

Dillinger yanked the pull chain; nothing happened. He flicked both switches on the wall. One turned on the light. The other did nothing.

'Mexico is not like the United States,' Rivera said.

Dillinger moved to open the french windows and nodded towards a table on which stood a pitcher of iced water and several glasses.

'Help yourself. If you don't mind, I'll have a wash.'

When Dillinger took his jacket off, Rivera noticed the underarm holster and gun with interest. No wonder the man could act with such authority. So much the better!

Dillinger put the holster down within easy reach. This Rivera looked rich. Dillinger trusted rich people less than poor people.

He stripped to the waist, poured lukewarm water from a pitcher into the basin on the washstand in one corner and sluiced his head and shoulders.

Rivera said, 'If you have not been to Mexico before, I recommend you order bottled water, Senor. American stomachs do not like our water.'

Dillinger nodded his thanks. Rivera sat down in a wicker chair by the table and Dillinger walked to the window, towelling his damp hair. A steam whistle blasted once, the sound echoing back from the mountains across the flat roofs, and a wisp of smoke drifted lazily into the sky from the station.

Rivera put down his glass and said, 'I'd like to offer you a job, Senor Jordan.'

'What kind of a job?' Dillinger was amused. This guy certainly didn't know who he was.

'I've re-opened an old gold mine near my hacienda at Hermosa. That's a small town in the northern foothills of the Sierra Madre, towards the American border. Hermosa and the area around it is rough country. The peasants are animals and the Indians who work the mines . . .' He shrugged. 'But you will find this out for yourself. What I

46

need is a man of authority, who will work with me for six months or a year. Keep discipline. You know what I mean?'

This guy was fascinating, Dillinger thought. 'Who keeps discipline for you now, Mr Rivera?'

'Ah,' Rivera said. 'I had a good man, also an American, very tall, very strong. He didn't want to go back to the States, the police bothered him there, and so he had an accident and now I have to replace him. I hope with you.'

'In one sentence,' Dillinger said, 'not a chance.'

'You have not heard my terms, senor. Two thousand dollars in gold for six months, five thousand dollars in gold for a year.'

Dillinger was really tempted to tell this fancy jerk that he'd made that much in five minutes by vaulting over a counter and emptying a teller's drawer.

'En oh,' Dillinger said. 'That spells no. But how would you like to work for me while I am in Mexico? You could be my guide. I'll pay you a thousand dollars for a month, how's that?'

Anger blazed in Rivera's dark eyes. The jagged white scar that bisected the left cheek that Dillinger hadn't paid attention to before seemed to stand out suddenly against the brown skin. Rivera took a cigarillo from his breast pocket and lit it. When he looked up, he had control again.

'I know you did not mean to insult me, Senor. You do not know the ways of Mexico.' He took a slow puff. 'I usually get what I want, Senor Jordan. We have a saying: *A man must be prepared to pay for past sins.* I will pay you double what I paid the other American if you return to Hermosa with me. My final offer.'

'Thanks, but no thanks,' Dillinger said gently. 'I'm really here on a kind of vacation.'

He was aware of the sweat trickling from his armpits,

soaking into his shirt and poured himself a glass of iced water, then remembered Rivera's warning.

Rivera said calmly, 'Your final word?'

'Yes. Sorry we can't do business.'

Rivera walked to the door and opened it. 'So am I, Senor Jordan. So am I.'

He closed the door behind him and descended the wide wooden stairs to the lobby and went outside. He found the old man who was guarding Dillinger's convertible sitting on the bench, a small bottle of tequila in hand. So, he'd spent some of the money already.

'Hello, Fallon, I thought I recognized you. Having a difficult time of it lately?'

The old man looked at him sourly. 'You should know, Mr Rivera!'

'You needed a lesson, my friend,' Rivera said, 'but that's history now. You can come back and work for me at Hermosa any time you like.'

'That's not work, Mr Rivera. It's slavery.'

'As you choose. Who is this Senor Jordan?'

'Jordan?' The old man stared at him blankly. 'I don't know any Jordan.'

'The one you were talking to. He owns the automobile. Who is he? What's his game?'

'I ain't telling you a damn thing,' Fallon said.

Rivera shrugged, walked along the terrace. Two men were sitting at the end table eating *frijoles*, a bottle of wine between them. One was a large, placid Indian with an impassive face, great rolls of fat bursting the seams of his jacket. The other, a small, wiry man in a tan gabardine suit, his sallow face badly marked from smallpox, got to his feet hurriedly, wiping his mouth. 'Don Jose.'

'Ah, my good friend, Sergeant Hernandez.' Rivera turned and glanced towards Fallon. 'I wonder if you might consider doing me a great favour?'

Hernandez nodded eagerly. 'At your orders, as always, senor.'

Twenty minutes later, Fallon surfaced with a shock as a bucket of water was hurled in his face. One side of his face hurt from his eye to his jaw. He was lying in the corner of a police cell. The big Indian who stood over him must have hit or kicked him. Fallon's side hurt as much as his face. Sergeant Hernandez sat on the bunk. Fallon recognized him instantly and went cold.

'What is this? What have I done?'

'You are a stupid man,' Hernandez told him.

'I'm an American. You have no right to put me in here,' Fallon said.

'If you don't like our ways, why don't you go back? You want me to escort you to the border and turn you over to your Federalistas?'

Fallon shook his head.

'You are here because to go back there you have to spend fifteen years in jail, is that not so?'

The massive Indian moved within kicking distance of Fallon on the floor.

'You see,' Hernandez said, 'he only knows one thing, kicking.'

Fallon rolled away from the Indian, which brought him closer to Hernandez.

Hernandez leaned down and whispered to him, 'I think you will now stop being stupid. Now I think you may even try to be sensible? Is this not so?'

'Sure,' Fallon muttered.

The cell door opened and Rivera entered. He glared down at Fallon.

Hernandez said, 'Senor Rivera has some questions to put to you. You will answer them. You understand?'

'Yes,' Fallon moaned.

'Excellent.' Rivera said and sat on the bunk. 'Let's start again then. This man, Harry Jordan. Who is he?'

A slight wind lifted the edge of the dingy lace curtains in Dillinger's room. The place had that strange, derelict air common to rooms in cheap hotels the world over. It was as if no one had ever really lived there. As Dillinger lay on the bed, he heard the great bell of the church toll, and it reminded him of Sunday mornings in Indiana when he was twelve. He'd led his neighbourhood gang – all sixth-grade boys – in a foray to steal coal from the Pennsylvania Railroad and sell it to the women in town. He remembered the happy days in Gebhardt's pool hall, and the even happier times playing baseball. He loved it because it was two games being played at the same time, winning against the other team, and being watched by the girls, who always went after the boys who had played best immediately after the game. Some of those older girls had terrific figures, not like these Mexican women. Jesus, was he getting homesick so soon?

He had to wait it out till the hunt for him cooled off. He had to be steel, like the time he found strength to pour acid on his heel in prison so he could get transferred to yard duty. They owed him nine years! He remembered how good he felt – like he was flying – when he got out of jail that first time. He wasn't going to spend any more time ever behind bars.

The knock on the door stopped his reverie. He hoped it was the damn bellboy with the bottled water he'd asked for more than an hour ago. God, things moved slow in Mexico!

'Come in,' he yelled. 'The door's open.'

What came in wasn't the bellhop but a small wiry man in uniform with a pock-marked face.

'Police, senor,' pock-marks said. 'I am Sergeant Hernandez. May I see your passport?'

Dillinger looked across the room to the dresser where his Colt automatic lay in its holster. The sergeant followed his eyes.

Dillinger swung his feet off the bed, went to his jacket, took out the Harry Jordan passport and handed it to Hernandez, who went through it page by page, his face expressionless.

'How much did you pay for this passport, Senor Jordan?' Hernandez asked.

'Same as anyone else,' Dillinger said.

'I must have you accompany us to headquarters, senor.'

'Would you mind explaining what this is all about?'

Hernandez straightened, his jacket falling open, and drew a revolver from the holster on his left hip. 'Please, senor, let's be sensible about this. No fuss, eh? We must think of the reputation of the hotel.' He pulled Dillinger's Colt automatic from its holster and pocketed it. 'We can drive to police headquarters in my car, or my driver can follow us in your car in case you do not wish to leave that beautiful automobile unattended in front of the hotel. You see, the man who was watching it, he is no longer watching it because he is in jail. Like you, Mr Dillinger, he doesn't want to be turned over to the Federalistas on your side of the border.'

4

In the courtyard a troop of Mexican Federal cavalry was exercising. Dillinger, with Hernandez beside him, waited till he could drive the convertible into the courtyard. He wasn't about to leave it in the street.

When he parked, Hernandez held his hand out for the keys.

Dillinger started to separate the trunk key from the ignition key on the ring.

'Both keys, Senor Jordan,' Hernandez said. 'If you please.'

Dillinger decided not to make a fuss about the trunk key. Considering what was in the trunk, he'd just as soon not call attention to it.

Inside, Dillinger was told to sit down on a rough wooden bench in the white-washed corridor, watched over by Hernandez's Indian. Through the open window, he could hear the shouted commands to the cavalry. If he had to shake loose of this place, he wasn't going to leave the convertible behind, which meant he'd have to be able to get it out of the courtyard. He'd get his keys back or he'd wire the ignition. Getting into the trunk would be a bitch. He was beginning to be sorry he hadn't left the car in the street and gotten a second set of keys made to keep under the bumper as he used to back home.

He stood up to make sure nobody was bothering the

52

car, but the Indian put a heavy hand on his shoulder and made him sit back down.

'Nobody does that to me,' he said uselessly. The Indian didn't understand him. 'You're going to be sorry you were born.'

Finally he heard a murmur of voices from down the hall and Hernandez beckoned to him. They passed many doors, Hernandez leading, the Indian behind, until they came to a door that was open, as if they were expected. Hernandez gestured, and Dillinger went in.

The office was sparsely furnished with two chairs and a desk and there was a rush mat on the floor. The one luxury was the ancient fan which revolved listlessly in the ceiling.

The man behind the desk wore a rumpled khaki uniform. He was middle-aged and balding, a small black moustache brushing his upper lip. When he smiled, Dillinger saw that most of his teeth had been capped in gold.

'I am Fidel Santos, Chief of Police,' he said in English. 'Please sit down, Senor Jordan.'

On the desk before him he had Dillinger's wallet and the false passport.

'What's all this about?' Dillinger asked.

'As with most things in life it is a question of money, senor.' Santos nodded and Hernandez placed a small black suitcase on the desk and flipped it open revealing the neat rows of bank notes. 'Just over eleven thousand American dollars, to be precise. We found it in the trunk of your car.'

Bastards, Dillinger thought.

'How have you earned this money, senor?'

'My father died three months ago and left me a small farm in Kansas which I sold.'

Hernandez stood by the window cleaning his nails with a knife. He paused and looked across. Dillinger was aware of the Indian behind his chair, of the faint creaking of the fan in the silence.

Santos said, 'You know that there is a government tax on foreign currency brought into this country?'

'No, I didn't know that.'

'Strange. According to your passport, you crossed our border at Solernas. One would have thought the customs officials there would have made this plain to you when you declared the money.'

There was another slight silence. Hernandez finished cleaning his nails, snapped the blade shut and slipped the knife into his pocket. Outside, a bugle sounded and the cavalry clattered across the cobbles into the plaza.

They seemed to be waiting for him to make the next move and Dillinger said, 'No one is sorry about this little misunderstanding more than I am. I'll be glad to pay the necessary tax to the proper authorities.'

'Unfortunately there is the question of the fine,' Santos said.

'All right, I'll pay the fine and put it down to experience.'

'I'm afraid that won't be possible, senor,' Santos said patiently. 'In such cases it is usual for the entire sum involved to be forfeited and then, of course, there is the question of a fine.'

Dillinger thought, these guys are thieves in uniform. He could feel the blood rising to his face. He had to keep his control.

'And how much would the fine be?' Dillinger asked.

'A difficult question in your case, senor. You see there is also the matter of certain firearms discovered under the rear seat of your automobile. Another serious infringement of our laws almost certainly leading to their confiscation and also of the vehicle itself.'

That hit Dillinger between the eyes.

He managed to keep control of his voice as he said, 'Folks, we have a saying in the States. You can take every-

54

thing away from a cowboy except his horse. That automobile is my horse.'

There was a pause.

Then Santos said, 'Perhaps you don't realize the position you are in. A prisoner at present in custody here, an American just like you, insists that your name isn't Jordan at all. Does that surprise you?'

Dillinger managed to look astonished. 'You've got my passport, haven't you?'

'Passports, senor, may be bought. Oh, I'm sure this is a nonsense, of course. The man concerned is an old drunk. He insists that you are the bank robber, John Dillinger, who recently escaped from prison in Indiana.'

Dillinger worked his way from an expression of total bewilderment to one of outraged laughter. 'Jesus, this guy must be out of his head.'

Santos laughed sympathetically. 'A drunken old fool, as I said. I foresee no problem in clearing the matter up, but you will, of course, have to remain in custody until we have an opportunity to check our *compadres* to the north.'

There was silence. Santos lit a cigar and nodded to the Indian. The Indian touched Dillinger on the shoulder and motioned him toward the door.

The Indian took Dillinger out and along the corridor and down a flight of stone steps to an iron door outside which a guard was sitting reading a newspaper. He unlocked the door.

The room was about forty feet square, with only one small window high in the opposite wall, and contained twenty or thirty other prisoners. Through the door came the strong odour of urine, human excrement and stale sweat. The Indian pushed Dillinger inside and shut the door with a clang.

Most of the prisoners were Mexicans in ragged trousers, shirts and straw sandals. Several of them came crowding round to look at the strange new prisoner. Someone touched his jacket. He felt a hand slide into his pocket. Dillinger grabbed for the wrist and twisted it with an easy strength that sent the man staggering across the cell. The others moved back a respectful distance. He pulled a drunk from a bench against the wall, sat down and lit a cigarette, hoping it would counter the stench around him.

There was more to this situation than met the eye, he thought, more even than Santos confiscating the money to keep for himself. If he'd wanted to do that, it would have made more sense to let him go.

A man got up to relieve himself in an overflowing bucket in the corner. The stink was terrible.

'Spare a butt, Mr Dillinger?'

Fallon eased on to the bench beside him. A livid bruise stretched from the corner of one eye to the edge of the jaw.

Dillinger shook a cigarette out for him. 'What did they use, a sledgehammer?'

'Sergeant Hernandez has an Indian sidekick called Valdez.' He rubbed his jaw. 'Built like the side of a house.'

'You told them I was John Dillinger.' It was a statement of fact, not a question. Dillinger sat there staring at Fallon calmly and the old man said, 'They made me tell them, Mr Dillinger, beat it out of me.'

Suddenly there was a scuffle between two prisoners on the bench next to theirs. Dillinger stood and with a voice that cut through the commotion like a sword shouted, 'Shut up!' Nobody needed to know what the words meant. The two scuffling prisoners returned to their places. The others stared at the *gringo* who spoke with an authority not even the chief of police had. Now when they talked, it was in whispers.

'That's better,' Dillinger said.

56

Fallon coughed. 'I saw you with that man Rivera. Do you know who he is?'

'He offered me a job at his mine.'

'He's the original walking bastard, that guy. When I first skedaddled into Mexico one step ahead of the cops, I went to work for Rivera.'

'You told him who I was.'

'I kind of let it slip that there was more to you than the name Jordan, but I wouldn't tell him no more than that.'

'Then the cops picked you up?'

'They sure did. Beat the hell out of me, then Rivera came in the cell and Hernandez said I'd better start talking or else. I had to agree to go back on the payroll at Hermosa, too. I didn't have a choice.

'That's OK, old timer.' There was one more cigarette in the pack. Dillinger broke it in two and offered him half.

Fallon put his half in his wallet.

'Saving it for later?'

'Saving it forever. What a souvenir, half a cigarette given me by Johnny Dillinger.'

'What's that?' Dillinger asked, pointing to a picture postcard that came partway out of Fallon's wallet as he put the cigarette half away for safekeeping.

Fallon unfolded the card. It was an advertisement for a hotel called Shanghai Rose. Standing in front of it was the most exotically beautiful woman Dillinger had ever seen.

'Who's that?'

'That's Rose herself. Runs the hotel in Hermosa now that her mother and father are both gone.'

'What makes her look that way?' Dillinger asked.

'You mean the eyes? She's half Chinese, half Spanish.'

'Is she as good looking in person as on that card?'

'Better. And a nicer woman you never met. It's hard to believe she's Rivera's niece. Her father and Rivera never got on. Rivera didn't want his kid brother marrying a Chinese woman. If he hadn't, there wouldn't have been

Rose. Last year when her father died, Rivera wouldn't go to the funeral. You know what she did, just to rub his nose in things? She had a new sign painted. Had them hang it above the front door of the hotel.'

'What's it say?'

'Shanghai Rose.'

Dillinger laughed out loud.

'Every time Rivera goes into town he sees that sign. Oh that Rose, she's something special.'

'You're not sweet on her, are you now?'

'Me?' Fallon said. 'She's a lady. Sides, she wouldn't look at anyone's as decrepit as me. In Hermosa, she's like a princess waiting for a prince to come along.'

Dillinger thought they'd have come for him by now. Fallon had dozed off. Now that he was waking up, Dillinger asked him, 'Why does Rivera have such trouble getting help for the Hermosa place?'

'The mine's a death trap. Least five cave-ins I know of. Christ knows how many dead Indians. He uses Apaches up there.'

'Apaches? I thought they went out with the old West.'

'Not in Sierra Madre. That was their original stronghold. Still plenty around up there.'

'If it's that bad, why'd you agree to go back? Why not cut and run when they let you out?'

Fallon shrugged. 'I don't have a *centavo* more than the change for the five dollars you gave me. In this country a *gringo* without money in his boot . . .' He shrugged.

The door opened and Hernandez looked in. 'Senor Jordan, will you come this way please.'

Dillinger picked his way between the Mexicans and followed Hernandez. They mounted the stone steps, passed along the whitewashed corridor and paused outside the office. Hernandez knocked and motioned Dillinger inside.

58

The air was heavy with the aroma of good cigars. Santos had one clamped firmly between his teeth. He took it out and grinned cheerfully. 'Ah. Senor Jordan. Sit down. I am happy to tell you that your troubles are over.'

Dillinger hardly noticed him. He had eyes only for Don Jose Manuel de Rivera as he turned slowly from the window and smiled. 'We meet again, Senor Jordan.'

'Seems so.'

'I am pleased Don Jose has employment to offer you,' Santos said, smiling. 'He has agreed to pay the balance of your fine out of his own pocket.'

'I came the moment I heard at the hotel that you'd been arrested,' Rivera said.

'That was real kind of you.'

'After speaking with Senor Santos it occurs to me that you may now review my earlier offer of employment in a somewhat different light.'

'I think you could say that.'

'Then you will be prepared to accompany me to Hermosa on the evening train?'

'What about my car?'

Rivera turned to Santos. 'It is his pride.'

'Mexico,' Santos said, 'has a generous heart. Senor Jordan may have his beautiful white automobile, without its arsenal, of course.'

Rivera picked up the passport. 'I will see that this is returned to Senor Jordan at a more suitable time.'

'Of course, Don Jose. I regret, however, that in the matter of the confiscated money, the law must take its course. However, in the circumstances and as Senor Jordan is now, as it were, in your custody, we will say no more about the fine.'

'How will I get my car to Hermosa if I go with you?' Dillinger asked.

'As I do with mine,' Rivera said. 'It travels on the flatbed railroad car reserved for automobiles. You are then prepared?'

Dillinger thought, I am prepared to see if Shanghai Rose is as beautiful as her picture. If she hates this son-of-a-bitch as much as I do, we ought to get along real fine.

5

Dillinger was amused by the idea that, for a change, he was being taken for a ride. With all the coal he'd stolen from the Pennsylvania Railroad, he'd never travelled any distance on a train before. Just an hour out he'd had the crazy idea of getting into his convertible on the flatbed and staying in it for the rest of the train ride because a car was a natural place for him to be.

The train was fun. He was following the conductor along the narrow corridor of the Pullman car and had to brace himself every couple of steps as the train swayed and rocked. The attendant knocked on a compartment door, opened it and moved inside.

There were two bunks, but Rivera had the place to himself. A small table had been pulled down from the wall and the remains of the meal were on it.

'Come in Jordan.'

He obviously intended a master and servant relationship and the dropping of the 'senor' was merely the first step. Dillinger leaned against the door and took out a packet of Artistas. The Mexican poured cognac into a glass, held it up to the light and sipped a little.

'So I'm Jordan again?' Dillinger said.

'I should have thought that the sensible thing for everyone concerned,' Rivera said. 'Your true identity is of no consequence to anyone but me.'

'Fallon knows.'

'Fallon will do exactly as he is told.'

'And that chief of police, Santos?'

Rivera smiled faintly. 'He has the money. I have his silence.'

'The money was mine,' Dillinger said.

'And from whom did you appropriate it? Let us concentrate on the future, not the past,' Rivera said. 'I needed a man to take charge of a rather difficult mining operation. A hard man to keep those Indians of mine in order. A man who is capable of using a gun if necessary. I should have thought you and your experience would fit the bill admirably.'

'Has it occurred to you that I might have other plans?'

'Hermosa is twenty miles from the nearest railway and there is a train only once a fortnight. The roads, I am afraid, are the worst in Mexico. However, we are linked to civilization by an excellent telegraph line and Santos did assign you to my care. If you misbehave, Santos is prepared to fill the last part of our bargain.'

'And what is that?'

'To turn you over to the American authorities at a border crossing – under your real name, of course.'

Dillinger dropped his cigarette into Rivera's brandy glass.

Anger flared in Rivera's eyes. 'Do your work, that's all I want from you. Do it well and we shall get along. Do it badly . . .'

Dillinger opened the door and went out. In a way, he'd won. In the end it had been the Mexican who had lost his temper.

The second-class coach was crowded, mostly peasant farmers going to market, and the great heat, heavy with the stench of unwashed bodies, was not the way Dillinger liked to travel.

He spotted Fallon in a corner by the door, playing patience with a pack of greasy cards. Fallon looked up, his face wrinkling in disgust. 'It's enough to turn your stomach in here, Mr Dillinger.'

'Which explains the second-class tickets,' Dillinger said. 'He wants us to know exactly where we stand.' He pulled his two suitcases from under the table. 'Let's get out of here. There's plenty of room in the first-class end. Another thing, it's Jordan, not Dillinger. Remember that.'

'I'll try,' Fallon said.

They went into the first empty compartment they came to. Fallon produced two bottles of beer from his canvas grip, and sprawled in the corner by the window.

'This is more like it. What do we do if the conductor comes?'

'What do you think?'

Fallon opened one of the bottles and passed it across. 'What did Rivera want?'

'Mainly to let me know who's boss.'

'He must be the great original bastard of all time.'

Dillinger tried the beer. It was warm and flat, but better than nothing. He put the bottle on the floor, lit a cigarette and placed his feet on the opposite seat.

'How come Rivera survived the revolution? I thought men like him were marched straight to the nearest wall.'

'I guess some did, some didn't. Some fish always escape the net.'

Dillinger awakened with a start. The train had begun the cautious descent of a narrow canyon, the coaches lurching together as the engineer applied the brake. Dillinger's watch said 4 a.m. He got up quietly and went past the sleeping Fallon into the corridor.

He stood by the window and shivered slightly as the cold mountain air was sucked in. The sky was very clear, hard white stars scattering towards the horizon, and a faint luminosity was beginning to touch the great peaks that towered on either side. A moment later the canyon broadened and he could see the lights of a station.

He heard Fallon behind him saying, 'La Lina – only a whistle-stop for mail and passengers. Another couple of hours to where we're going.'

'I didn't even know we'd passed through Chihuahua.'

'Didn't seem any point in waking you. We were only there for twenty minutes while they changed the engine.'

La Lina swam towards them out of the darkness as the train coasted in and slowed to a halt. There was a small station house with a couple of shacks behind it and nothing more. The station-master came out carrying a lantern, and three Mestizos in straw hats and blankets, who had been crouching against the wall, got to their feet and came forward.

Fallon and Dillinger jumped to the ground and walked towards the rear of the train. A couple of box cars had been linked on behind the flat car on which the Chevrolet had been roped into place. When they paused to light cigarettes they heard a low whinny and the muffled stamp of hooves.

'When did they join us?' Dillinger said.

'Chihuahua. The guard told me they were thorough-breds going up to Juarez for the races next week.'

When they turned to retrace their steps the three Mestizos were standing patiently beside the train, hands in the air, while the station-master and guard searched them thoroughly.

'What's all that about?' Dillinger said.

'They say that the train's been robbed three times in the last four months,' Fallon told him. 'Bandits get on at way-stations dressed like dirt farmers. Last year in Sonora they shot the engineer of the night express and left it to freewheel down a gradient. Ran off the track after five miles.'

They boarded the train again and the guard closed the

door. He turned and said in English, 'I notice, senors, that you have moved into a first-class compartment.'

Dillinger replied, 'It's too crowded in the other coach.'

'It is also cheaper, senor. You are prepared to pay the necessary addition?'

'Now there you put me in a delicate position,' Dillinger told him.

The guard shrugged and replied with perfect politeness, 'Then I'm afraid I must ask you to resume your former seats. I have my duty – you understand?'

'I knew it was too good to last,' Fallon said.

They got their cases from the compartment and moved back into the second-class coach. Most of the occupants were sleeping and they sat down in their original seats in the corner by the door which led to the luggage van.

Fallon laid his head on his arms. Dillinger tilted his hat forward, saw a young Indian girl in a red skirt, a large cloth bundle on the floor between them. She stared past him into the wall, blindly, as if in a trance.

He finished his cigarette and closed his eyes. A few moments later he was aware of the girl moving. He glanced up and saw that she was looking back along the coach at the three Mestizos who had boarded the train at La Lina. One of them nodded briefly.

The man removed his blanket and stood up. He was of medium height, broad shoulders bulging beneath the faded khaki shirt, and the Indian blood showed in the high cheekbones and broad nose.

The girl went forward without a word, placed her bundle on the table and untied it. The three men immediately reached inside and took out revolvers. Dillinger nudged Fallon with his elbow.

'Hey, this is terrific. We've got company.'

Fallon sat up and cursed softly. 'Well, I'll be damned. Juan Villa.'

'You know him?'

'Used to be one of Rivera's peons. Stuck his knife into a foreman a couple of years back. A real firebrand. You ever hear of Pancho Villa?'

'Sure.'

'Juan claims to be his nephew. Bullshit, but it goes down big with the peasants.'

On seeing Fallon, Villa's face was illuminated by a smile of great natural charm. He raised a hand warningly as his two companions went towards opposite ends of the coach.

'You would be wise to place your guns on the table, old friend,' he said in halting English. 'It would desolate me to have to kill you.'

'We aren't armed,' Fallon told him.

'Then stay where you are and don't try to interfere.'

He raised his revolver and fired once through the roof. The effect was astonishing, a sudden eruption of sleeping passengers, a stifled scream, then frightened silence.

'We will now pass around the hat,' Juan Villa said. 'You would do well to contribute generously.'

Dillinger thought banks were a helluva lot better than trains. Less risk, more loot. Maybe Mexico didn't have enough banks.

The door beside Dillinger opened and the conductor stepped in. He hesitated for no more than a second before turning to run – too late. The bandit who had been standing at that end of the coach shot him in the back.

Now that's not sporting, Dillinger thought.

A child screamed and its mother placed a hand over its mouth. In the passage between the coach and the baggage car the conductor was moaning. Dillinger started to his feet.

These guys are doing it all wrong.

Immediately the barrel of Villa's revolver swung towards him and Fallon cried out frantically, 'No, Juan, no!'

Villa hesitated and then shrugged. 'I owe you a favour.

66

This cancels it.' He turned to the bandit who had shot the conductor. 'Lock them in the baggage car and come back.'

Fallon gave Dillinger a shove. 'Get moving!'

The conductor had stopped groaning. They stepped over his body. The bandit bent down to pick up the bunch of keys the man still clutched in his right hand, then followed them into the baggage car.

'Stinking *gringos*,' the bandit said. 'A bullet in the head is better, I think.' He threw down the keys and thumbed back the hammer of his pistol.

'Villa won't like that,' Fallon cried in a panic.

'So I tell him you tried to jump me.'

The bandit pushed the barrel of his revolver into Dillinger's back. Dillinger had practised the manoeuvre a hundred times. He had anticipated a policeman's gun in his back, marching him somewhere he didn't want to go. Dillinger raised his hands, pivoting on his left foot, his left arm coming down on the man's gun arm as Dillinger's right hand, now formed into a fist, continued the movement by smashing into the side of the man's face. With his left arm tight around the bandit's gun hand, Dillinger raised his left arm up sharply, hearing the crack of bone. The man dropped the revolver and collapsed with a groan.

Instantly, Fallon grabbed the gun up from the floor.

'You stay here,' Dillinger said. 'I'll work my way back to the Pullman car. See if we can catch them between two fires.'

Dillinger opened the door and the cold air sucked the door outwards, sending it crashing back against the side of the coach. The train was moving at no more than twenty miles an hour and he stepped out on the footboard, reached for the edge of the roof and pulled himself up.

There was a catwalk running along the centre and he worked his way to the end of the baggage car and sprang across to the roof of the second-class coach. The stars were pale and in the east the dark peaks were already tipped with fire as he jumped to the roof of the Pullman and lowered himself down through the open window to the door.

When he reached Rivera's compartment he knocked softly. It opened almost immediately. Dillinger pushed Rivera back in and stepped inside.

Rivera had obviously just awakened. 'What is it?'

'Bandits got on at La Lina. We're having a little trouble back there. Have you got a gun?'

Rivera looked at him suspiciously, then pulled a suitcase from under his bunk, opened it and produced a revolver. 'How many bandits?'

'There were three, but Fallon's looking after one of them in the luggage van. The leader's a man called Villa. Fallon said he used to work for you.'

'Juan Villa?' Rivera's face hardened. 'That man is a murderer!'

He brushed past Dillinger and moved along the corridor quickly. The noise of the train effectively cloaked any disturbance that was taking place inside the second-class coach as they passed through the empty first-class compartments. Rivera paused at the door to listen for a moment, then opened it.

Juan Villa was halfway along the coach, his hat held out to a group of people at a table. The third man stood with his back to them a couple of feet away. Rivera took a quick step forward and placed the barrel of the gun against his neck. The man's whole body seemed to go rigid and Rivera plucked the revolver from his hand and passed it to Dillinger.

He moved forward and said, 'Villa!'

Villa looked up sharply. For a moment his face was clean of all expression and then he smiled. 'Eh, *patrón*. We meet again.'

'Put down the gun,' Rivera said.

As the bandit hesitated, Dillinger shouted to Fallon. A

moment later, the first bandit lurched in from the luggage van holding his head, Fallon behind him.

Villa shrugged and dropped his gun on the table.

'Take them to my compartment,' Rivera said.

Fallon pulled the young Indian girl up from the end table and pushed her after the others. 'She was in it, too.'

'What about the conductor?' Dillinger said.

'Dead.'

As they reached Rivera's compartment, the engineer sounded the steam whistle three times, the emergency signal, and braked sharply.

The train slowed to a halt and Dillinger looked out of the window. A bunch of steers were milling across the track, a dozen or fifteen peons on horseback vainly trying to urge them on. Suddenly they turned and galloped forward with shrill cries, drawing revolvers and firing as they came. When they reached the train they dismounted.

Dillinger ducked back inside and turned to Villa. 'Friends of yours?'

The bandit grinned. 'I don't think they're going to like the way you've been treating me, amigo.'

There was an outburst of firing from the rear of the train. A mounted trooper galloped past the window and then another. Rivera pushed Villa forward. 'Three times they've made this trip to Juarez, my friend. They were beginning to lose faith in you.'

Dillinger looked out and saw mounted troopers of the Federal cavalry emerging one by one from the box cars at the end of the train. Most of the bandits were still trying to remount when they were surrounded. They tried firing back, but it was no use. They were outmanoeuvred and outnumbered. It was all over.

Rivera pulled on his jacket and turned to Fallon. 'You stay here with Villa. If he makes the slightest move to escape, shoot him.' He nodded to Dillinger. 'Bring the others outside.'

As he jumped to the ground, the young officer in command of the troop walked forward and saluted. 'Lieutenant Cordonna. They informed me in Chihuahua that you were travelling on the train, Don Jose. It would seem we have been completely successful.

'Not quite,' Rivera said. 'They murdered the conductor.'

'Which one is Villa?'

'He is at present under guard in my compartment. He, of course, must be held for public trial in Chihuahua, but the others . . .'

Cordonna shouted to his sergeant. 'Bonilla, how many have you?'

'Fifteen, Lieutenant.'

Cordonna looked at the two bandits from the train. 'These also?' Rivera nodded and pushed them forward. 'What about the girl?'

Dillinger swung round quickly. 'She's only a kid.'

'Like all Americans you are a sentimentalist,' Rivera said. 'I would remind you that it was the girl who carried the arms on board, relying on the fact that she wouldn't be searched. She is directly responsible for the conductor's death.'

Cordonna grinned. 'What a pity. I could find a better use for her.' He sent her staggering towards Bonilla. 'Six at a time. Detail ten men.'

The windows of the second-class coach were crowded with faces, but there was no sound as the troopers pulled carbines from their scabbards and dismounted. They marched the bandits a little way from the train and lined up the first six on the edge of a small hollow.

Cordonna strolled toward them, paused and barked an order. The sound of the volley echoed back from the mountains.

Cordonna and Sergeant Bonilla drew their revolvers and moved forward as two of the fallen started to scream.

Dillinger glanced at Rivera's impassive face, then looked across at the Indian girl.

Dillinger turned, climbed up into the train and went along to Rivera's compartment. Villa was sitting on the bunk and Fallon lounged in the doorway, the barrel of his revolver propped across his left forearm.

'I'll take over here,' Dillinger said.

'If you think I'm going to get any pleasure from watching that bunch outside you're mistaken.'

'Then go and have a smoke or something. I'd like a word with our friend here.'

'Suit yourself,' Fallon said, and went away along the corridor.

Out of the silence, as Villa and Dillinger looked at each other, Cordonna's voice drifted, sharp and clear on the morning air. There was no fear on Villa's face, only strength and a blazing intelligence.

'In case you have failed to discover the fact for yourself, I should inform you that the *patrón* enjoys this sort of thing.'

'He called you a murderer.'

'Quite true, senor. He had a foreman at his hacienda and I had a young wife who killed herself. It did not take me long to discover the reason. It seemed to me that I was justified in putting my knife between his ribs. The *patrón* thought otherwise.'

'I thought it would be something like that.' The silence was broken by another volley and Dillinger moved out into the corridor and opened the door on the other side. He turned to Villa. 'You'd better get going. You haven't much time.'

'For what, a bullet in the head, senor?'

Dillinger took the remains of his packet of Artistas from his pocket and tossed it across. 'You can keep them.'

Villa's face split in a wide grin. 'Sometimes God looks

71

down through the clouds, senor. It is almost enough to give a man faith again.'

He jumped down to the ground and ran for a narrow gully that curved up into the scrub that covered the lower slopes. Dillinger watched him disappear, then broke the revolver and emptied the rounds into his hand. He threw them away and turned as the third volley crashed out.

A moment later Rivera climbed up and immediately frowned at the sight of the open door. 'What has happened?'

'I'm afraid Villa got away,' Dillinger said.

Cordonna appeared in the doorway at ground level and stood there listening. Rivera said, 'Why didn't you shoot him?'

'I tried to.' Dillinger took the revolver from his pocket and handed it across. 'Unfortunately, the damned thing wasn't loaded.'

As he turned from the rage in Rivera's eyes, Cordonna ran for his horse, calling to his men. Dillinger moved along the coach between the staring people and sat down beside Fallon.

'What's all the excitement?' Fallon asked.

'Villa got away.'

As the train moved forward with a sudden jerk, Fallon said, 'Johnny, I kind of think you and that fellow you just let get away have a few things in common.'

6

Dillinger had had enough of the train to last him. 'I can't wait till they get my Chevvy on the ground again,' he told Fallon. 'I want to pay my first call on what's her name — Rose — the lady at the hotel.'

'First may be last if Rivera catches you. He doesn't like his people consorting with his enemies.'

Dillinger grabbed Fallon by the front of his shirt. 'Don't ever refer to me as one of his people. I don't belong to anybody.'

'I'm sorry,' Fallon said. 'Meant no harm.'

Dillinger released him. 'Let's get one thing straight, Fallon. You're an American and I'm an American and nobody else around here is an American, which gives the two of us some common ground that's one helluva lot more important than the fact that we are temporarily working for Rivera.'

'What do you mean temporarily, Johnny?'

'Do you intend to stay? I don't intend to stay. Your problem is you can't go home and you need some dough to live on this side of the border, right?'

Fallon nodded.

'I intend to solve your problem just as soon as I solve my problem. My problem,' Dillinger continued, 'is that you blew my cover.'

'You know I didn't want to.'

'Some people who talk lose the use of their tongues.'

73

'But Rivera knows.'

'Well,' Dillinger said, 'he might just lose something else.'

'What might that be?'

'The thing he values most.'

'His life?' Fallon asked.

'His gold.'

'We're almost there,' Fallon said to Dillinger, who was getting more and more restless by the minute.

In the far distance a feather of smoke marked the train's progress and a faint whistle echoed back eerily. The only signs of man's presence were the telegraph poles that branched from the railway line, marking the rough track which led over the lower slopes of the mountains to Hermosa.

The canyon floor was a waste of gravel and rock, bright in the morning sun, dotted with clumps of mesquite and sage. Already the fierce heat of this dead land was beginning to rise from the ground.

At the station, Rivera took charge of the flurry of activity, getting the luggage off, then supervising the unloading of the convertible.

'Tell them anybody scratches the paint on that car is going to get personal retribution from me,' Dillinger told Rivera.

'You better learn some Spanish,' Rivera said, 'because as soon as we get to the mine, you're going to have to give your own orders.'

'*Avanca*, hurry your ass, *vamos*, let's go, *vete*, get out of here. See,' Dillinger said, 'Fallon's been teaching me real good.'

As the Chevvy was driven down the ramp and came to rest on the solid but dusty ground, Dillinger patted the hood as if it was the nose of a horse. He unscrewed the hood ornament and topped up the water in the radiator, then seated himself behind the wheel as if it was a throne.

'He is a child,' Rivera said to Fallon.

'I wouldn't let him hear you say anything like that, Senor Rivera,' Fallon whispered.

Just then a large buckboard came over the hill, pulled by two horses. Its iron-bound wheels rattled over the stones in the dirt road.

The driver was an ox of a man. Under his wide-brimmed straw hat was a coarse and brutal face. A revolver and cartridge belt were strapped to his waist. He jumped to the ground and hurried forward, hat in hands.

'You're late, Rojas,' Rivera said. 'I've been waiting for at least half an hour.'

'There was trouble at the mine, *patrón*,' Rojas said in his harsh voice.

'Anything serious?'

'I took care of it.' Rojas held up a fist like a rock.

'Good,' Rivera said. 'You got my wire?'

Rojas nodded and glanced at Dillinger. 'Is this the one?'

Rivera said, 'Senor Jordan will operate under my direct orders when circumstances require it. You, Rojas, will still control the men.'

It was part of Rivera's plan never to let just one man be in charge of disciplining the work in the mine. Rojas would seek his favours as he did in the past. And the *gringo* would keep Rojas on his toes – as did the *gringo* before him. Rivera ruled by the oldest precept of all: divide and conquer.

'Hey,' Rojas shouted, spotting Fallon, 'the old fool has come back.' He strutted over to Fallon, only to find Dillinger barring his way.

'The old fool's name is Mr Fallon. My name is Mr Jordan. Your name is?'

'Rojas!' Rojas shouted.

'Pleased to meet you, Senor Rojas,' Dillinger smiled, extending his hand.

'Enough of this nonsense,' Rivera said. 'Get the buckboard loaded. We've wasted enough time.'

Dillinger and Fallon stooped to raise one of the packing cases between them. Rojas, to show off, lifted the other easily in his great arms.

'We haven't got all day to waste while you two fool about like a couple of old washerwomen.'

He pushed Fallon out of the way, grabbed at the packing case and tried to pull it from Dillinger's grasp. Dillinger held on tight, and with the point of his right boot caught the Mexican on the shin where a small blow will go a long way. Rojas staggered back with a curse. Dillinger lifted the packing case into the buckboard and turned to face him.

'Sorry, I didn't see you there,' he said calmly.

The Mexican took a single step forward, his great hands coming up, and Rivera cried, 'Rojas — leave it!'

Rojas reluctantly stepped back, eyes smouldering. 'As you say, *patrón*.'

'Follow us with the buckboard, Rojas.' Rivera said. He got into the rear seat of the convertible as Fallon slipped in beside Dillinger at the wheel. As they went over the brow of the hill above the railway line, Dillinger offered Fallon a cigarette.

The old man said in a low voice, 'What are you trying to do — commit suicide?'

'Rojas?' Dillinger shrugged. 'He's like a slab of granite. Hit it in the right spot and it splits clean down the middle.'

'I hear everything you say,' Rivera said from the back seat.

'I intended you to hear it,' Dillinger replied, winking at Fallon.

Dillinger knew that few men would survive a real brawl to the finish with Rojas. But that in itself was a challenge, something a man like Fallon would never be able to understand. You don't protect yourself from a bully by kissing his ass.

Dillinger leaned back in the seat, the heat of the day enfolding him, narrowing his eyes. Already the mountains were beginning to shimmer in the haze and lose definition. As they progressed higher into the sierras, they passed through the tortured land of mesas and buttes, lava beds and twisted forests of stone, a savage, sterile land that, without its gold, was no place, Dillinger thought, for a good, clean-living bank robber.

'I've got six cans of gas in the trunk,' Dillinger shouted to Rojas over the roar of the engine, 'but it won't last for ever. Where do you get gas out here?'

'You get it from me,' Rivera said. 'There is a tank at the hacienda.'

Dillinger made a mental note to get some of that spare gas secreted somewhere. He didn't want the oats for his horse in Rivera's exclusive control.

'We haven't passed another car,' Dillinger said.

'You miss the traffic back home?' Fallon said.

'The paved roads is what I miss,' Dillinger said, laughing. To Rivera he shouted, 'When's this road going to get paved?'

'When hell freezes over,' Fallon said low enough so that Rivera couldn't hear, and they both laughed.

'What are you two laughing at?' Rivera asked.

They both shrugged their shoulders at the same time. That made them laugh again, and only aggravated Rivera more. As far as he was concerned, all Americans were just grown-up children.

An hour later they came round the shoulder of a mountain and saw an immense valley, a vast golden plain, so bright with heat it hurt the eyes to look at it. At the side was a great hog's back of jagged peaks lifting into the clear air, incredibly beautiful in their savagery.

'The Devil's Spine,' Fallon said, 'is what they call it.'

'Looks more like an impregnable fortress,' Dillinger said.

'That's what it was in the old days. They say there's a ruined Aztec or Pueblo city somewhere on top.'

Then the shot rang out, its sound dying away quickly. Dillinger instinctively jammed on the brakes. Shading his eyes with both hands, he examined the landscape.

Rivera said, 'Probably a hunter.'

'Hunter my ass,' Fallon whispered.

Two Indians came over the hill riding small wiry ponies. They wore red flannel shirts and breech-clouts, almost like a uniform, their long hair held back with bands of red flannel. Both of them carried rifles in the crooks of their arms. One of them held the carcass of a small deer across his blanket saddle.

'I told you it was a hunter,' Rivera said.

'Hunting for him' Fallon whispered.

The Indians came down the slope. Instead of reining in their ponies, they let the animals crowd the stopped car, as if getting a message across.

Dillinger started to inch the convertible forward. One of the Indians raised the barrel of his rifle slightly.

'We don't want any trouble with these now,' Rivera said, but Dillinger noticed in the rear-view mirror that Rivera had slid his revolver out of his waistband onto the car seat beside him. Dillinger felt naked without his Colt.

Suddenly a voice called out, high and clear in a language Dillinger was not familiar with, and a third rider came over the rim of the hill and moved down towards them fast and the two Indians backed off slightly.

The new arrival reined in beside the Chevrolet and sat looking at Rivera, a fierce Indian with a wedge-shaped face that might have been carved from brown stone. He wore his black hair shoulder length under a shovel hat of

78

the kind affected by some priests, and a faded black cassock, pulled up to his knees, revealed untanned hide boots.

There was a silence, dust rising in small whirls as the ponies danced. Rivera had turned quite pale. He sat there staring back at the man, a muscle twitching in his jaw. The Indian returned the gaze calmly, the sunlight slanting across his slate-coloured eyes and then he abruptly turned his pony and went galloping away, followed by his companions, leaving the Chevvy in a thin cloud of dust.

'One day I shall kill that animal,' Rivera said, as Dillinger shifted gears and resumed speed.

'He didn't look like a man it would be too easy to kill,' Dillinger commented.

'Filthy Apache,' Rivera said.

'Name's Ortiz — Juan Ortiz,' Fallon said. 'His people call him Diablo. Ever come across Apaches before?'

Dillinger shook his head. 'Only in the movies.'

As Dillinger drove, Fallon filled him in.

'I guess you don't know too much about Apaches. Even their name means enemy. In the old days what they really lived for was war, against other tribes, against the settlers, against anybody. The ones in the States have been pretty much tamed. Lot of them shipped off to Florida somewhere. But the ones who came back down here . . . you don't want to tangle with them. Ortiz was what they call a Broncho Apache, the kind that stick to the old ways. When he broke his back in a riding accident, he ended up in the mission hospital at Nacozari. The Jesuits started educating him.'

'Madness,' Rivera interjected.

'Now he's a kind of lay brother or something,' Fallon went on. 'Works with the priest in Hermosa, Father Tomas. I think the old man would like the Indian to take his place when he's gone.'

'Over my dead body,' Rivera shouted. 'Ortiz is a Chiricahua Apache, cruellest savages that ever set foot on God's earth.'

'Geronimo was a Chiricahua,' Fallon said. 'It's only forty-five years since the American cavalry chased him right into these mountains and forced him to surrender.'

'They should have been exterminated,' Rivera said. 'Every last one of them.'

'He's doing a pretty good job of that right now up at the mine,' Fallon whispered.

Rivera glared at them. 'What are you whispering?'

'Don't get paranoid,' Dillinger said. 'Just two Yankees shooting the breeze.' To Fallon he said, 'The Indians at the mine are Apaches?'

Fallon nodded. 'Mainly Chiricahua with a sprinkling of Mimbrenos.'

'Where'd you learn all this?'

'From Chavasse. He's only a kid, mid-twenties, I'd guess, but he knows more about Apaches than any man I know. Came here from Paris to write a book about them and ended up being manager of Rose's place.'

'Ah, Rose's place,' Dillinger said.

A moment later they topped a rise and saw Hermosa in the valley below. There was a single street of twenty or thirty flat-roofed adobe houses, with a small whitewashed church with a bell tower at one end. The hotel, clearly visible, was the only two-storeyed building in the place.

Ragged, barefooted children ran after the Chevrolet, hands outstretched for coins. Rivera tossed some loose change to scatter them as the Chevvy pulled up outside the hotel. On the crumbling façade, eroded by the heat of the desert, was a weathered board sign: SHANGHAI ROSE.

They climbed down and Rivera said, 'I've had enough of this damned heat. I'll go out to the hacienda in the cool of the evening.' He preceded them inside.

Fallon said to Dillinger, 'I hope he doesn't run into Rose first thing. They hate each other's guts.'

'Come on,' Dillinger said, 'I need to wet my whistle.'

Inside there was no sign of Rivera. Fallon led the way into a large stone-flagged room. There were tables and chairs and a zinc-topped bar in one corner, bottles ranged behind it on wooden shelves. A young man poured beer into two glasses.

'Lord God Almighty's just been in to tell me you were here. He's gone up to his room,' he said in English with a pronounced French accent.

Fallon picked up one of the glasses and emptied it in one long swallow. He sighed with pleasure and wiped his mouth with the back of one hand. 'Another like that and I'll begin to feel human again. André Chavasse, meet Harry Jordan.'

They shook hands and the young Frenchman put two more bottles on the counter and grinned. 'We heard you were coming, courtesy of Rivera's telegraph. All the comforts of civilization, you see.'

He was perhaps twenty-five, tall and straight with good shoulders, long black hair growing into foxtails at his neck. He had a handsome, even aristocratic face. The face of a scholar that was somehow relieved by the mobile mouth and humorous eyes. A man it would be hard to dislike.

Dillinger turned to Fallon. 'What happens now?'

Fallon shrugged. 'I suppose he'll want us at the mine tomorrow.'

'Where do we stay?'

'Not at the hacienda, if that's what you're thinking. Rivera likes to keep the hired help in their place. There's a shack at the mine.'

'You're staying here tonight,' Chavasse put in. 'Rivera booked the room. It's the brown door at the top of the stairs.'

Dillinger swallowed his beer and put down the glass.

81

'If it's all right with you, I'll go up now. I feel as if I haven't slept in two days.'

Fallon grinned at the Frenchman. 'We had ourselves a rough ride in. Villa and his boys tried to take over the train, then we ran into Ortiz on the way in. That didn't improve Rivera's temper, I can tell you.

'You saw Ortiz?' Chavasse asked eagerly. 'How did he seem?'

'Had blood in his eyes, if you ask me. One of these days Rivera's going to do something about him.'

'I would not like to be Rivera when that day comes,' the Frenchman said gravely.

'You think he's dangerous?' Dillinger asked.

Chavasse took a cigarette from behind his ear and struck a match on the counter 'Let me tell you something, my friend. When you speak of the Apache you speak of the most dangerous fighting men who ever walked the face of the earth. Rivera will find one day that he has pushed Ortiz once too often.'

'And André should know,' Fallon said. 'He's forgotten more about Apaches than I'll ever know.'

'Right now,' Dillinger said, 'the only thing I'm interested in is about eight hours' sleep and whatever passes for a bath around here.'

He walked out into the dark hall and paused to remove his jacket, blinking as the sweat ran into his eyes. A step sounded on the porch and a spur jingled as someone entered.

He turned slowly. A young woman stood in the doorway looking at him, the harsh white light of the street outlining her slim figure. Booted and spurred, she wore Spanish riding breeches in black leather, a white shirt open at the neck and a Cordoban hat.

But it was her face that blinded him: slightly oriental eyes that were unusually large, the nose tilted, a sensuous mouth. There was about her a tremendous quality of repose, of tranquillity almost, that filled him with a vague irrational excitement.

'You are Senor Jordan?' she said. 'Harry Jordan, who is to run the mine for my uncle? I am Rose Teresa Consuela de Rivera.'

She removed her hat revealing blue-black hair, plaits coiled high on the back of her head. She put out her hand in a strangely boyish gesture and he held it for a moment, marvelling at its coolness.

'You know, for the first time I actually feel glad I came to Mexico,' he said.

The look that appeared on her face lasted for only a second and then she smiled. Laughter erupted from her throat and the sound of it was like a ship's bell across water.

7

It was evening when Dillinger awakened. The coverlet had slipped from him in his sleep and he lay there naked for a moment watching the shadows lengthen across the ceiling before swinging his legs to the floor. The window to the balcony stood open and the curtains lifted in the slight breeze.

The courtyard at the rear of the hotel seemed deserted when he peered out, and he quickly filled the enamel basin on the washstand with lukewarm water from a stone pitcher, went out onto the balcony and emptied the basin over his head.

He towelled himself briskly, pulled on his pants and shirt, then examined his face in the cracked mirror, running a hand gingerly over the stubble of beard. He opened one of his suitcases, took out razor and soap and got to work.

There was a knock at the door and as Dillinger turned, wiping soap from his face, Rivera entered. He carried Dillinger's shoulder holster and the Colt .32. He dropped them on the bed.

'Well, the world is full of surprises,' Dillinger said.

'There are eight rounds in there, my friend, as you know. If we have trouble with Ortiz, do you think eight rounds are enough?'

Dillinger twirled the Colt around once by the finger

guard. 'One round is enough. Eight can be too few. Depends on the circumstances.'

'Am I wrong to trust you?'

'You are wrong to trust anybody.'

Rivera laughed. 'Here are some pesos in case you want to indulge yourself in the saloon downstairs. It is not a gift, but an advance against your pay. Don't lose it at poker.'

'I don't lose at poker,' Dillinger said, 'or anything else. What about gas for my car?'

'I trust you with a gun because I have two and I have Rojas. But I do not trust you yet with gas that would give you ideas of leaving Hermosa. Perhaps you will learn to ride a horse, Americano,' Rivera said, laughing again as he closed the door behind him.

Somewhere, someone was playing a guitar and a woman started to sing softly. Dillinger put on the shoulder holster, finished dressing, brushed back his hair and went outside.

Rose de Rivera leaned against the balcony rail at the far end of the building, her face towards the sunset as she played. In Chicago, he had once heard a woman singing in Spanish in a night spot, but nothing like this. Rose's voice was as pure as crystal.

His footfall caused her to turn quickly, the sound of the last plucked string echoing on the evening air in a dying fall. She wore a black mantilla and a scarlet shawl draped across her shoulders. Her dress of black silk cut square across the neck. A band of Indian embroidery in blue and white edged the bodice.

She smiled. 'You feel better for your bath?'

'You saw me?'

'Naturally, I turned my back.'

'My compliments on the dress. Not what I'd looked for.'

'What did you expect, a *cheong sam*? Something exotically Chinese? I wear those, too, if I'm in the mood, but tonight the Spanish half of me is what I feel.'

'Are you more proud of your Chinese half or your Spanish half?'

'When I am feeling Chinese, I am proud to belong to an ancient and wise civilization except for one thing.'

'What's that?'

'They invented gunpowder,' she said, and she came close. He didn't know what to expect, but all she did was touch his side where the shoulder holster showed. 'Who are you?' she said.

'What about your Spanish half?' he said, avoiding the question.

'My father used to tell me a Rivera sailed with the Spanish Armada.'

'Didn't they lose against the English?'

'Is winning always everything?'

'The Americans beat the English.'

'You are all terrible, vain, proud, impossible. What do you do for a living when you are not being strongman for my uncle? You know he is only playing you off against Rojas?'

'Yes.'

'You know what happened to the last American who worked for him?'

'Yes.'

'You think God gives you special protection that others do not have?'

'Yes,' he said, laughing.

'You haven't answered anything I've asked you. Why are you being so mysterious?'

Dillinger thought how different she was from the push-overs back home. If he'd seen her in Indiana he'd have thought of her as a stranger. His girlfriend, Billie Frechette, was part Indian, really a dish, but nothing like Rose.

He kissed her lightly, the way he'd seen in the movies,

keeping his chest away from her so she wouldn't feel the holster pressing against her. When he kissed Billie, she always put her hand down there right away, but Rose just smiled and turned away just enough so he wouldn't try again.

For a second he thought it was his heart beating loudly, but it was a drum pulsating through the dusk, and voices started an irregular chant, the sound of it carried towards them on the evening breeze. There was a flicker of flame from a hollow about a hundred yards away and he noticed an encampment.

'Indians?'

'Chiricahua Apaches. They sing their evening prayer to the Sky God asking him to return the sun in the morning. Would you like to visit them? We have time before supper.'

A flight of wooden stairs gave access to the courtyard and they moved out through the great gateway and went towards the camp. Rose took his arm and they walked in companionable silence.

After a while she said, 'Fallon told me about how my uncle tricked you. He is a hard man.'

'That's putting it mildly. How do you and he get on? Your uncle would like to see you go?'

'My presence is a continual irritation. He's offered to buy the hotel many times.'

'But you don't want to leave?'

She shook her head. 'When I was twelve my father sent me to convent school in Mexico City. I was there for five years. The day I returned, it was as if I had never been away.'

'Why should that be?'

'This countryside,' she said, 'it's special. I don't like cities. Do you?'

'Not too much,' he said.

'You are lying to please me.'

He wanted to tell her that out in the countryside the banks were far apart and didn't have all that much money lying around. You had to go to the towns and cities for the big loot.

'In Mexico the people make heroes of their bandits. In the States, they make heroes of gangsters.'

Was she guessing? Did she know something?

'Your uncle,' Dillinger said, 'is a bigger bandit than Villa.'

'Yes,' she said, laughing, and took his hand, but just for a moment. He felt desire again, and hoped it didn't make him crazy in the head the way it used to, the longing he couldn't stand.

'In the countryside here,' she said, 'have you noticed that the rocks shimmer, the mountains dance, and everything is touched with a blue haze? I think the countryside is like the face of God. Sometime we are not meant to see too clearly.'

Her hand was on his arm, an unmistakable tenderness in her voice. He looked down at her and she flushed and for a moment her self-assurance seemed to desert her. She smiled shyly, the evening light slanting across her face, and he knew that she was the most beautiful woman he had ever seen.

There was something close to virginal fear in her eyes and this time he squeezed her hand. Her smile deepened and she no longer looked afraid, but completely sure of herself.

Without speaking, they turned and moved on towards the encampment. There were three wickiups, skin tents stretched tightly over a frame of sticks, grouped round a blazing fire. Three or four men crouched beside it singing, one of them beating a drum, while the women prepared the evening meal.

Several children rushed forward when they saw Rose,

but stopped shyly. She laughed. 'They are unsure with strangers.'

She moved towards them and the children crowded round, wreathed in smiles. She spoke to them in Apache, then beckoned to Dillinger. 'There is someone I want you to meet.'

She led the way to the largest wickiup. As they approached, the skin slap was thrown back. The man who emerged looked incredibly frail. He wore buckskin leggings, breech-clout and blue flannel shirt, a band of the same material binding the long grey hair.

The face was his most outstanding feature. Straight-nosed, thin-lipped, with a skin the colour of parchment, there was nothing weak here, only strength, intelligence and understanding. It could have been the face of a saint or a great scholar. By any standards he looked like a remarkable man.

Rose bowed her head formally, then kissed him on each cheek. She turned to Dillinger. 'This is my good friend, Nachita — last chief of the Chiricahuas.'

Dillinger put out his hands in formal greeting and felt them gripped in bands of steel. The old man spoke in surprisingly good English, the sound like a dark wind in the forest at evening.

'You are Jordan, Rivera's new man.'

'That's right,' Dillinger said.

Nachita kept hold of his hands and something moved in his eyes like a shadow across the sky. The old man released his grip and Dillinger turned away, looking out across the camp.

'This is quite a place.'

Behind him, Nachita picked up a dead stick and snapped it sharply, simulating the distinctive click of a gun being cocked. Dillinger reached for the gun under his arm, turned crouching, the Colt in his hand as if by magic.

Nachita smiled, turned and went back into his wickiup.

His lesson was for Rose. Here was a man who handled guns as if they were his hands.

Dillinger found Rose watching him, her face serious, the firelight flickering across it. He laughed awkwardly and put the gun away.

'He certainly has a sense of humour,' Dillinger said.

There was a pause as she looked at him steadily and then she said, 'We must go back to the hotel. Supper will be ready.'

Dillinger took her arm as they left the camp. 'How old is he?'

'No one can be sure, but he rode with Victorio and Geronimo, that much is certain.'

'He must have been a great warrior.'

They paused on a little hill beside the ruined adobe wall and Rose said, 'In 1881 Old Nana raided into Arizona with fifteen braves. He was then aged eighty. Nachita was one of the braves. In less than two months they covered a thousand miles, defeated the Americans eight times and returned to Mexico safely, despite the fact that more than a thousand soldiers and hundreds of civilians were after them. That is the kind of warrior Nachita was.'

'Yet in the end the Apache were defeated, as they were bound to be.'

'To continue fighting when defeat is inevitable, this requires the greatest courage of all,' she said simply.

Funny she should say that. He'd imagined himself one day coming into a bank he'd cased but not too well and finding himself in a trap, every teller a G-man waiting with a gun instead of a wad of bills. He'd imagined himself backing out of the bank, shooting machine guns from both hips, knocking out the G-men like ducks in a gallery. He'd walked out of three movies where he could tell that the gangster was going to get killed in the end.

After supper Dillinger went into the bar and joined Fallon,

90

who was sitting with Chavasse at a small table in the corner. Fallon produced a pack of cards from his pocket and shuffled them expertly.

'How about joining us for a hand of poker?'

'Suits me.' Dillinger pulled forward a chair and grinned at the Frenchman. 'Shouldn't you be working?'

Rose arrived, carrying bottles of beer and glasses on a tray. 'My manager is permitted to mingle with special guests,' she said.

'As always, your devoted slave,' Chavasse said dramatically, grabbing her hand and kissing it with pretended passion.

She ruffled his hair and disappeared into the kitchen.

Dillinger felt a sting of jealousy. He said, 'She just introduced me to old Nachita. Quite a guy.'

Chavasse said, 'Everything that's best in a great people. He taught me more than anyone else about the Apache.'

'Fallon tells me you're quite an expert on the subject.'

The Frenchman shrugged. 'I studied anthropology at the Sorbonne. I decided to do my field work for my thesis as far away from home as I could get. I meant to stay six months. But where in Paris could I get a job like this?' He laughed. 'And such a nice boss.'

Dillinger felt the sting again, wondered if there was some kind of a relationship between the Frenchman and Rose. She had ruffled his hair as if it was nothing.

When they had finished their beer Dillinger took some of Rivera's pesos from his pocket and slapped them on the table. 'How about another round?' he said to Fallon.

'With pleasure,' the old man replied.

Dillinger lit a cigarette and leaned back in his chair. 'This man we met on the road today, the one they call Diablo? Juan Ortiz. What do you make of him?'

'I honestly don't know. When he was younger, he had a bad reputation. They say he killed at least three men. Knife fights, things like that. There isn't much law in the mountains. I think in the old days he'd have made a name for himself, but that was before the Jesuits at Nacozari got their hands on him.'

'And you really think he's changed?'

'What was your impression?'

Dillinger frowned, thinking about it. 'I got the feeling he was trying to provoke Rivera in some strange way. It was almost as if he was inviting him to lose control.'

'But why would he do that?' Chavasse asked.

'I don't know. Maybe to give him the excuse to strike back.'

'This is a country saturated in blood. First the Aztecs, then the *conquistadores*. In four hundred years, nothing but slaughter.'

'Yet you stay.'

'I stay.'

As Fallon returned with the beer, Dillinger spied Rivera sitting down at a small table. He wore clean clothes and smoked one of his usual cigarillos. When he rapped on the table with his cane, Chavasse got up and went across. He listened to what Rivera had to say and went into the kitchen. He returned with a tray containing a bottle of champagne and a glass. He placed them in front of Rivera and came back to the others.

'Champagne?' Dillinger said blankly. 'Here?'

'Kept especially for Lord God Almighty,' Chavasse explained. 'One of his favourite ways of publicly indicating the gap between himself and others.'

At that moment Rojas swaggered into the bar, looking as if he'd been drinking. When he saw Rivera he pulled off his hat and bowed respectfully. Rivera called him over and murmured something to him. Rojas nodded and after a moment crossed to the bar and hammered on it.

'What about some service here?'

Before Chavasse could get up, Rose appeared from the kitchen. She walked round the counter and stood facing him, hands on hips. 'In the first place lower your voice. In the second take that thing off and hang it in the hall with the others.' She pointed to the revolver strapped to his waist.

Rojas turned meekly and went outside. He came back without the revolver and she placed a bottle of tequila and a glass on the counter.

Rojas filled his glass with tequila and swallowed it down, the spirit slopping out of the corners of his mouth. Dillinger looked at Rivera, who returned his gaze coolly, filled his glass with champagne and sipped a little.

Dillinger drank some of the lukewarm beer and put the glass down firmly. 'How much is that champagne?'

'Twenty-five pesos a bottle,' Chavasse said.

Dillinger, pulled off his right boot and extracted a folded bank note from under the inner sole. He pulled the boot back on and flicked the note across to the Frenchman.

'Twenty dollars American. Will that do?'

'I should imagine so.'

'Then get a bottle and glasses. Ask Rose to join us.'

Chavasse looked at Rivera and grinned, pushed back his chair and went into the kitchen.

'There goes my mad money,' Dillinger said ruefully.

Chavasse hurried back, followed by Rose with the champagne and glasses on a tray. Suddenly everyone seemed to be laughing and there was an atmosphere of infectious gaiety. Dillinger glanced at Rivera, the Mexican returned his gaze.

'To the provider must go the honour of opening it,' Fallon said.

As Dillinger reached out, a shadow fell across the table. Rojas pushed Chavasse out of the way and wrapped a huge hand about the bottle. 'I always wanted to try this stuff.'

Dillinger grabbed the neck of the bottle firmly. 'Then go and buy your own.'

93

'Why should I, Yankee, when you are here to provide it for me?'

The Mexican tried to lift the bottle from the table. Dillinger exerted all his strength to keep it there. Rojas grabbed the edge of the table and tried to turn it over and Dillinger leaned his weight against it.

As Dillinger half turned in his chair, he had a glimpse of Rivera still sitting calmly on the other side of the room sipping champagne, only now there was a smile on his face and Dillinger knew that the whole thing had been arranged. Rojas imagining he was going to teach him his place on the *patrón*'s orders. Rivera intent on discovering just how good he was.

Rose took Rojas by the arm and tried to pull him away. 'Please,' she said. 'No fighting in my place.'

Rojas, his hand still on the champagne bottle, turned toward Rose and spat in her face.

Chavasse was livid. All Dillinger's repressed anger boiled up. A hard ball of fury rose in his throat, choking him. With a swift movement, he leaned back, removing his weight from the table and Rojas lost his balance, releasing his grip on the bottle as he sprawled on his hands and knees. Dillinger smashed the bottle across the back of the bull neck and stood up.

The others moved out of the way hurriedly. Rojas shook his head several times and started to get up. Dillinger snatched up his chair and smashed it across the great head and shoulders once, splintering it like matchwood.

Rose was crying, wiping her face.

Rojas shook his head, wiping blood from his face casually. He got to his feet, his eyes never leaving Dillinger.

He stood there swaying, apparently half out on his feet, and Dillinger moved in fast. Rojas took a quick step backwards, then smashed his bull fist savagely into Dillinger's face.

Dillinger lay on the floor for a moment, his head singing

94

from the force of the blow. Rivera laughed and as Dillinger started to his feet, Rojas delivered a powerful blow to his stomach and hit him again on the cheek, splitting the flesh to the bone.

Rojas came in fast, boot raised to stamp down on the unprotected face. Dillinger grabbed for the foot and twisted, and Rojas fell heavily across him. They rolled over and over, and as they crashed against the wall, Dillinger pulled himself on top. He reached for Rojas's throat and was suddenly thrown backwards.

As Dillinger scrambled to his feet, Rojas rose to meet him. Dillinger feinted with his left and smashed his right fist against the Mexican's mouth, splitting the lips so that blood spurted. He moved out of range, then feinted again and delivered the same terrible blow. As he stepped back, his foot slipped and Rojas got home a stunning punch to the forehead that sent Dillinger staggering back against the open window to the boardwalk outside and he almost went over the low sill. As he straightened up, Rojas lurched forward again. Dillinger ducked, twisted a shoulder inwards and sent the Mexican over his hip through the open window in a savage cross-buttock.

Dillinger scrambled across the sill, almost losing his balance, and arrived on the boardwalk as Rojas rose to his feet. Dillinger, enjoying the best fight he'd had since he was a kid, hit him with everything he had, full in the face, and Rojas went backwards into the street.

For a little while he lay there and Dillinger hung on to one of the posts that supported the porch. Slowly, the Mexican got to his feet. He swayed in the lamplight, his face a mask of blood, eyes burning with hate, and then his hand went round to the back of his belt. As he came forward, a knife gleamed dully.

Behind Rojas, old Nachita appeared from the darkness like a ghost. His hand moved in a single smooth motion and a knife thudded into the boardwalk at Dillinger's feet.

There was a mist before Dillinger's eyes and he felt as if he had little strength left in him. He picked up the knife and went toward Rojas, the knife held out in front of him.

He heard a voice say, his own voice like that of a stranger, 'Come on, you bastard. If that's the way you want it.'

Rojas, who had been prepared to fight knife to hands not knife to knife, stumbled away into the darkness.

Dillinger swung round, the power in him like a white-hot flame. They were all there on the boardwalk, looking at him strangely in the lamplight, fear on their faces. Rivera stood at the top of the steps and Dillinger went forward, the knife extended.

Rivera staggered back, almost losing his balance, and hurried into the hotel. Dillinger was aware of a grip of steel on his arm. Old Nachita took the knife from him, supporting him at the same time, and Rose appeared on the other side.

She was still crying and Dillinger couldn't understand why. As they led him forward, he frowned, desperately trying to concentrate, and then as they reached his room, Fallon appeared and got the door open, his face ablaze with excitement.

'Jesus, Johnny, I never seed anything like that in my whole damn life. You really took that big ox apart.'

'Johnny?' It was Rose's voice. 'I thought your name was Harry. Who are you?'

He turned to her voice, smiling foolishly, and tried to speak and then the lamp seemed to revolve into a spinning ball that grew smaller and smaller and finally disappeared into the darkness.

This time J. Edgar Hoover had only one operative standing in front of his desk. He'd just finished reading the man's report.

'You've got a pretty good fix on him.

The man said, 'He didn't do the California job or the Chicago job. The woman we picked up in Kansas swore she'd seen a white Chevvy convertible in Doc's barn. If Doc didn't take it to Florida, maybe Dillinger took it south.'

'You think it's Mexico.'

'Mr Hoover, if there was this scale manhunt on for me, I'd get out of the country.'

'OK. Send a wire to Mexico City. Ask them to query the chiefs of police in all northern provinces if a white Chevrolet convertible has been seen driven by an American. Ask them to keep it confidential. Just say the car is stolen and the man who's driving it is probably armed and dangerous.'

8

The desert was a dun-coloured haze reaching toward the mountains, the canyons still dark with shadow. It was the best hour of the day, the air cool and fresh before the sun started to draw the heat out of the barren earth.

Dillinger, behind the wheel of the Chevrolet, Fallon beside him, seemed to ache in every limb. He drove slowly over the rough trail to spare himself and because Rose was cantering along beside them on a bay horse.

'How do you feel?' Rose asked.

'I guess I'm not very handsome today.' The right side of his face was disfigured by a large purple bruise.

'Do you think it was worth it?'

He shrugged. 'Is anything?'

She said to Fallon, 'Do you think he tries to commit suicide often?'

'Only on his bad days,' the old man replied.

The trail wound its way between a forest of great tapering pillars of rock and entered a narrow canyon. In the centre it widened into a saucer-shaped bowl, then narrowed again before emerging once more into the plain.

At this point the track branched off in two directions and Rose halted. 'There is where I leave you. I'm going straight to the mine. Father Tomas is staying at the village for a few days and I promised to take him some medicine. Perhaps I'll see you later?'

Dillinger switched off the motor. 'I think maybe we should have a talk first.'

She sat there looking down at him and then nodded, 'All right.'

The horse ambled forward. Dillinger got out of the car and walked beside her, a hand on a stirrup. 'I hope you don't think I — well, you know, was too pushy last night.'

'As long as you understand that a kiss is not necessarily a promise of better things to come.'

'I'm used to, well, a different kind of woman.'

'You're blushing.'

'I don't blush,' Dillinger said sharply.

'Perhaps it is the sun,' she smiled. 'I think I'd better tell you something.'

He felt that jealous pang again. He was certain she was going to tell him that the Frenchman and she were involved.

'Harry — or Johnny — whatever your real name is —' She looked over at Fallon to make sure he was out of earshot. 'I was in the telegraph office first thing this morning. There's a police alarm out for a white Chevrolet.'

'From Santos or Hernandez?'

'To them, from the FBI.'

'Damn. Who knows about this?'

'The telegrapher. He hasn't seen your car. But he is paid by Rivera to tell him everything that comes in over the wire.'

'Are there police in town?'

'Two. Both old. They won't see the message if Rivera doesn't want them to. Why are they looking for you?'

'Not me. My car. I must have lent it to a bootlegger.'

'You are very charming when you lie.' She patted her whinnying horse's neck. 'Till later then. Perhaps I can put something on that poor face of yours.'

'What?'

'My hand,' she said, cantering away.

Half an hour later the white convertible came over a rise and the track dipped unexpectedly into a wide valley. Below them stood a brown-stone hacienda built in the old colonial style.

The place seemed prosperous and in good repair, with well-kept fences around a large paddock. A worker in riding boots and faded levis was saddling a grey mare. He turned and looked up at them, shading his eyes with one hand, then went towards the house.

Dillinger drove into the courtyard and pulled up at the bottom of the steps. As he got out, a little girl ran out of the front door, tripped and lost her balance. As she started to fall, he moved forward quickly and caught her.

She was perhaps three years old and wore a blue riding suit with a velvet collar and brass buttons. She was frail, her brown eyes very large in a face that was too pale for a land of sun.

Dillinger set her on her feet gently and a woman moved out onto the steps and gathered the child to her. 'Juanita, how many times have I told you?' She looked up at Dillinger. 'My thanks, senor.'

She was a slender woman with greying hair and a black dress buttoned high to the neck. She wore no jewellery and her face was lined and careworn, the eyes moving ceaselessly from place to place as if she was continually anxious about something.

As Dillinger removed his hat, Rivera appeared on the porch. He stood there looking at his wife, saying nothing, and she took the child by the hand and hurried inside.

Rivera turned to Dillinger. 'I'd intended coming with you to the mine, but there are matters I must attend to here first. Rojas is already there. He'll show you over the place. I'll be along later.'

He went back inside.

Too bad, Dillinger thought. If he'd known, Rose could have driven with them instead of taking the horse. She could have sat between him and Fallon up front, her left thigh against his right thigh.

Dillinger drove away, following Fallon's directions up out of the valley. The heat was increasing. He could feel the sweat from his back soak through his shirt.

Finally, they came over the crest of a hill and saw a valley below. Dillinger had seldom seen a more dismal sight in his life. There were perhaps twenty or thirty crumbling adobe houses with a dung heap at one end and what appeared to be an open latrine running straight through.

There was a well in the centre of the village and a woman was in the act of lifting a pitcher of water to the ground as they approached. She was in an advanced state of pregnancy, her belly swollen. She paused, obviously tired, and Dillinger got out of the car.

He took the pitcher from her and said, '*Donde su casa?*', surprising himself at the bits of Spanish he had picked up by just listening.

She pointed silently across the street. He walked before her and opened the door. There was only one room and it had no windows. It took several moments for his eyes to become accustomed to the half light. When they did he saw an old woman stirring something in a pot over a smouldering fire. A few Indian blankets in the corner were obviously used for bedding, but there was no furniture. He put down the pitcher, his stomach heaving at the smell of the place, and went outside.

'That place isn't fit for a dog to live in,' he said as he climbed back into the car. 'Isn't anyone doing anything for these people?'

'Rose does what she can. So does Father Tomas. He's the best friend they've got, but they're like zombies. Rivera has the men doing a fourteen- or fifteen-hour day. They're worked so hard they don't give a damn about anything any more.

Rose's horse was tethered beside a buckboard outside a house at the other end of the village and Dillinger braked to a halt.

'Is the mine far from here?'

'Just over the rise, three or four hundred yards.'

'You walk on up. I'll join you later.'

Fallon trudged away up the street and Dillinger approached the hut just as Rose, hearing the car, came out. She looked tired and pale and there was sweat on her face. Dillinger took the canteen from the Chevrolet and handed it to her. 'You don't look too good.'

'There's not much air in there, that's all.' She poured a little water into the palm of one hand and rubbed it over her face.

'Who's inside?'

'Father Tomas. I'd like you to meet him.'

Dillinger followed her in. The place was exactly the same as the other, the room half filled with acrid smoke from the fire of dried dung. A man lay on a filthy blanket in the corner, an Apache woman crouched at his feet.

A white-haired old priest sat beside him on a small stool, gently sponging the damp forehead. Dillinger leaned closer. The skin on the man's face was almost transparent, every bone clearly defined. He was obviously very ill.

The priest clasped his hands together and started to pray, his face raised to heaven, a single shaft of sunlight through the smoke hole lighting upon the white hair.

Dillinger made his way outside, Rose following him. From his pocket he took the flat bottle of tequila Chavasse had given him against emergencies and he unscrewed the cap and swallowed.

He turned to look at her. 'Can't anything be done?'

'My father had a plan, a wonderful plan. At the far end of the valley, above the hacienda where the streams run down from the snows of the sierras, he wanted to build

102

a dam. With its waters, the whole valley would have flowered.'

'And your uncle doesn't see things that way?'

'I'm afraid not, senor,' Father Tomas said, emerging from the house behind them. 'Don Jose is interested only in obtaining as much gold as these wretched people can squeeze from the mine. When he is satisfied that the well has run dry he will leave for what to him is a more favourable climate.'

'This is Senor Jordan, Father,' Rose said. 'The one my uncle forced into coming here.'

The old man took Dillinger's hand. 'I heard what happened in Hermosa last night, my son. God moves in his own good time. Perhaps Don Jose made a mistake when he tricked you into coming here?'

Before Dillinger could reply two horsemen galloped down the hill, one behind the other, and turned into the street. Rojas was slightly in front and he reined in so sharply that his horse danced sideways on its hind legs, crowding Dillinger, Rose and the old priest back against the wall, splashing them with mud.

His companion was a Mestizo in a battered red straw hat. A man who had turned against his own people. He had coarse, brutal features and a hide whip dangled from his right wrist.

Rojas sat there glaring at Dillinger. Two of his teeth were missing and his lips were twice their normal size. A livid green bruise stretched from his chin across the left side of his face to the eye, almost closing it.

'What do you want?' Father Tomas said.

'I've come for Maco. The swine's not turned up for work again.'

'He's too sick,' the old man said.

'They're always too sick.' Rojas dismounted. 'They know we need every available man at the mine and take advantage of it.'

He took a step forward and Dillinger put a hand against his chest. 'You heard what Father Tomas said.'

Rojas moved back and his right hand dropped to the butt of his revolver.

'I wouldn't do that if I were you,' Dillinger said calmly.

Through the stillness they could hear the rattle of the steam engine that operated the conveyor belt up at the mine and the thin, high voices of the Indians calling to each other. The Mestizo with the whip fidgeted nervously, avoiding Dillinger's eye. Rojas turned without a word, scrambled into the saddle and lashed his horse into a gallop.

Dillinger turned to Father Tomas and Rose. 'I think it's time I took a closer look at this mine.'

Rose climbed into the saddle of the horse. 'I'm returning to Hermosa now. Will you be coming in this evening?'

'You sure you want to keep company with a desperate character like me?'

'Perhaps I can make you see the error of your ways.'

'I doubt it, but I tell you what you can do?'

'What's that?'

'You can buy the champagne this time.'

She smiled, and he slapped the horse on the rump and it galloped away.

He drove out of the village, following the track up to a small plateau that was like a shelf in the face of the mountain. Water, splashing in a dozen threads from the snow-capped peak, had been channelled to run through a stoutly constructed shed, open at both ends.

It was a scene of great activity. Near the mouth of the mine, the old steam engine puffed smoke, drawing in a steel cable that hauled trucks laden with ore along a narrow track.

Dillinger got out of the Chevrolet and headed toward the ore shed. Fallon emerged to beckon him in. 'Come see this,' the old man said.

Inside the ore shed the only piece of machinery was a steam-operated crusher. Two Indians fed its flames with wood. The heat was unbearable. The water ran into a great tank lined against leakage with clay and there were several cradles and two puddling troughs. The Indians who worked at them were stripped to the waist, their bodies shining with sweat.

'Why doesn't he bring in more machinery? If the mine's producing anything like a return it would pay him.'

'I told you, they closed it in 1893 after the rock came down on more than fifty Indians. Since I've been here we've had so many cave-ins I've lost count. Men get killed all the time.'

'Then the timbering must be at fault. Don't tell me Rivera's trying to save money there, too?'

Fallon shook his head. 'The mountain's just waiting to come down on all of us. Every time you cough in the tunnel a rock comes down. That's why we daren't use any more machinery. The vibration might be all that's needed.'

They paused beside three wooden cabins and he opened the door of the first one. 'This is where we live.'

It was plainly furnished with table and chairs, two bunks and an iron stove in one corner.

'Who uses the other two?' Dillinger asked.

'One of them is the powder store. Rojas lives in the end one.'

'Where is he now?'

'Went into the mine about five minutes ago, looking like murder. I pity any poor devil in there who gets in his way.'

They walked beside the rails past the steam engine, and entered the mouth of the tunnel. Dillinger had expected it to be cooler in the tunnel. Instead, the heat was worse.

'What's wrong with the ventilation in here?'

'The air shaft was blocked by a rock fall a couple of months ago,' Fallon replied. 'Rivera gave orders to leave it alone and concentrate on bringing the ore out.'

'Hell, that sounds dangerous to me. Didn't you tell him that.'

Fallon shrugged. 'He said we hadn't got the time to waste.'

They turned a corner and the sunlight died, leaving them in a place of shadows illuminated by lanterns and guttering candles. When they reached a fork Fallon hesitated. 'There are two faces, north and south. Rojas could be at either.'

They stood to one side as a truck moved past them pushed by half a dozen weary, dust-coated Indians. Fallon lifted a lantern from a hook in the wall and led the way into the darkness.

Gradually, Dillinger was conscious of faint sounds, and a light appeared. The tunnel narrowed until they had to stoop and then it opened into a low-roofed cavern, badly illuminated by several candles.

Ten or twelve Indians crouched at the rock face swinging short-handled picks. Others gathered the ore into baskets, which they emptied into another truck. The air was heavy, thick with dust and almost unbreathable.

Dillinger turned away and moved back along the tunnel. He paused once, leaning against the wall, and coughed harshly, trying to clear the dust from his lungs. There was a sudden slide of pebbles from the darkness above.

'See what I mean?' Fallon said.

Dillinger didn't reply. He turned and moved back along the tunnel. Suddenly a man cried out in pain, the sound echoing flatly through the darkness.

Dillinger started to run, and gradually the light increased as he came out into the main tunnel and saw several Indians crouched against the wall, their truck tipped on to its side, ore blocking the track.

With one hand Rojas kept an old, grey-haired Indian down on his knees. In the other he wielded a whip. It whistled through the air and curved round the thin shoulders, drawing blood. The old man cried out in pain.

106

When the whip rose again, Dillinger spun Rojas round and sent him crashing back against the wall. The Mexican gave a cry of rage and came up from the floor, drawing his revolver.

Dillinger moved in fast, ramming one arm against the man's throat, grabbing the gun hand and forcing the barrel towards the floor. For a moment they swayed there and suddenly the revolver went off.

The sound re-echoing in the confined space was like a charge of dynamite exploding and the earth seemed to tremble. As the Indians cried out in alarm, the mountain rushed in on them.

9

Dillinger remembered thinking, 'This is it,' as everything seemed to cave in all around him. He'd thought that once before in a small bank, an easy job, and as he'd gone out the door carrying a bagful of bills he saw ten feet ahead of him a man too old still to be a cop pointing his .38 at him from a distance nobody could miss at. 'This is it,' he'd thought, but the policeman's gun clicked, a misfire, and Dillinger had kicked the weapon out of the cop's hand, jumped on the running board of the waiting car that took him on the grit road to safety. That was the time he decided never to do a job without the protection of a bullet-proof vest.

A bullet-proof vest, even if he'd had one on, is no protection against a mine cave-in. Dillinger lurched forward, groping his way through clouds of dust. He tripped and fell on his hands and knees. He lay there for a moment, coughing and choking, and then scrambled up a sloping ramp of rubble to where light gleamed between stones.

He pulled at them with his fingers and Fallon and Rojas appeared on either side of him, the Mexican obviously gripped by fear. A few minutes later the gap was wide enough and they crawled out into the sunlight followed by four Indians.

A crowd was already running toward them from the ore shed and Father Tomas came over the hill behind them in his buckboard. He reined in a few yards away and jumped to the ground.

'How bad is it?'

Fallon's face was a mask of dust. 'I think the whole damned mountain's fallen in.'

Dillinger took the bottle of tequila from his pocket, swallowed some and passed it to Fallon. Rojas was sitting on a boulder, his head in his hands, dazed. Dillinger handed him the bottle of tequila and said roughly, 'Get some of that down you and pull yourself together.'

Rojas took a long swallow, coughing as the fiery liquid burned into his stomach. He got to his feet and wiped his mouth.

'How many men are still inside?' Dillinger demanded.

'I'm not sure. Twenty or so.'

Fallon scrambled on top of the boulder and addressed the crowd in Spanish. 'Those men in there haven't got long. If we're going to do anything it's got to be now. Get pick-axes, shovels, baskets – anything you can lay your hands on.'

Dillinger and Fallon led the way up the slope and started to pull boulders away from the entrance. Everyone joined in, even the old priest, forming a human chain to pass the earth and stones backwards as they progressed farther into the tunnel.

The gap through which they had made their escape was widened until it would admit a dozen men with equipment. Lanterns were passed through and Dillinger stripped off his shirt and examined the wall of rock that filled the rear of the tunnel.

It was hot. The air was heavy with the settling dust. Fallon moved beside him. 'We've got to keep on digging. At least we've got the tools.'

Rojas crawled through the darkness to join them. He reached up and touched the ceiling. Immediately several flakes of stone peeled away.

'It wouldn't take much to bring down the rest.'

'We'll be all right if we're damn careful,' Fallon told him, trying to sound confident.

They laboured feverishly in the weird, dust-filled light, stripped to their waists, sweat glistening on their naked backs. Rojas proved to be a pillar of strength, his great hands lifting, unaided, rocks which Dillinger and Fallon would have found difficulty in moving together. Behind them a line of Indians formed up, passing back the baskets of stone and earth.

They worked in shifts, supporting the roof with fresh timbering as they advanced, but progress was slow. The lack of air and the great heat made it impossible for anyone to last for longer than half an hour at a time at the face. By the middle of the afternoon they were no more than forty feet into the tunnel.

Just after three, Rojas, in front, let loose a groan.

'What is it?' Dillinger demanded.

Rojas turned, the whites of his eyes shining in the lamplight. Dillinger crawled forward into the narrow cutting they had cleared into the heart of the rockfall. An immense slab of stone weighing at least five or six tons was stretched across their path.

Fallon crouched at his side and whistled softly. 'We haven't a hope in hell of moving that by hand.'

'What about dynamite?' Dillinger said.

Rojas sucked in his breath sharply. 'You must be crazy. Half a stick would be enough to bring down the rest of the mountain.'

'If there's anyone still alive back there they're going to die anyway,' Dillinger said. 'At least we'd be giving them a sporting chance.'

He crawled back along the tunnel past the line of Indians and emerged into bright sunlight. The whole village seemed to be there, women and children included, some

110

squatting on the earth, others standing as they waited patiently.

Dillinger thought, whoever thinks robbing a bank is dangerous ought to try this some time.

An Indian handed him a bucket of water and he raised it to his lips, drinking deeply before pouring the rest over his head and shoulders. Then he noticed Rivera.

'How bad?' Rivera asked.

'We've gone as far as we can with pick and shovel. There's a five-ton slab blocking our way.'

'Have you tried splitting it?'

'It would take hours by hand,' Dillinger said. 'Dynamite is the only answer.'

'It could also bring the whole place down.'

'Maybe, but there are at least twenty men in there according to Rojas. If we don't get them out within three or four hours they'll be dead.'

'You don't even know that they are alive now.'

'For Christ's sake, we've got to try,' Fallon said.

'He's right,' Dillinger said. 'They deserve some sort of chance.'

Rivera said, 'I am not going to destroy the source of gold to save a few Indians. You can try to reach them with pick and shovel. On no account will you use dynamite.'

'We'll see about that,' Dillinger said.

As Dillinger turned to go, he heard Fallon's 'Watch out!' Rivera had levelled the revolver in his hand at the back of Dillinger's skull.

'One false move and you're dead,' Rivera said. Then called out, 'Are you there, Rojas?'

'Yes, *patrón*.' Rojas had three Mestizos beside him now, all armed.

'Excellent. Now this is what I want. You, Fallon, get back into the mine and keep the men digging around the big slab. No dynamite!'

'Yes, senor,' Fallon said like a beaten man.

'As for you,' Rivera said to Dillinger, 'your friend Rojas will sit alongside you as you drive your pretty white car back to Hermosa where you will be turned over to the authorities, who will advise their American counterparts that they have captured the man in the white convertible. Understood? You are finished here.'

Dillinger looked around at what 'here' represented. A crowd of rescue workers and their women. Rose, watching him from less than fifty feet away helplessly. Next to her, in black, Father Tomas. And far behind them, standing on an outcrop of rock, Ortiz and two of his warriors.

Dillinger knew instinctively how men like Rivera control a community by their harshness in public. He would not hesitate to shoot 'as an example to others'. The easiest one to shoot and get away with was the big-shot *gringo* who was an escapee from the law in his own country.

To Dillinger's surprise, it was Father Tomas who came forward.

Immediately Rivera waved his revolver in his direction. 'Do not come closer, Father.'

Father Tomas did not miss a step until he was close enough to Rivera to touch him. He touched the left arm, the one without the gun, and said, 'Please, Senor Rivera, this man from America is right. We must try quickly to save the lives of those souls who are entombed in the mine. If the only way to work quickly is dynamite, let it be dynamite. If God wills, the men will be rescued alive.'

'And if God doesn't will, the mine will collapse and not another ounce of gold ore will be gotten out of there. Let go of my arm, Father. Tend to God's business, not mine.'

'Please, let the men be rescued,' Father Tomas said, 'and put that thing away.' He reached for Rivera's gun arm, and in that same instant, Rivera turned to face him and

112

point blank shot Father Tomas in
of the bullet sent Father Tomas b
people gasped and cried out.

'Rivera,' Dillinger said, 'you are a son o
coward.'

Rojas was about to strike Dillinger when a voice, louder
than the crash of thunder, was heard. It was Ortiz, standing on the rock with his two warriors. 'Rivera,' he
boomed, 'as God is my witness, you are a dead man!'

Ortiz and his men clambered off the rock, mounted,
and with a war cry as of old, galloped off.

As Dillinger drove slowly back to Hermosa, trying for the
second time in a month to hatch out an escape plan, he
could see that Rojas, sitting in the passenger seat, would
much rather find an excuse for drilling him than for turning him over to the authorities as Rivera had ordered.

Suddenly there was the sound of hoofbeats and catching
up with the car were Ortiz and his warriors on their
ponies. Ortiz's rifle was in his saddle, but he knew it was
useless to draw. The hated Rojas would kill the American
before Ortiz's bullet would reach Rojas.

'American,' Ortiz yelled. 'Rivera should let you use
dynamite. The men in the mine are my people,' the Apache
said. He dug his heels into his pony and went over the
ridge toward the village in full gallop.

'Catch up with him' Rojas ordered.

'I don't dare,' Dillinger said. 'The radiator's boiling.
Can't you see the steam. We have to add water.'

'You have a water can in the trunk?'

'Only gasoline.'

'Don't get nervous,' Dillinger said to Rojas. And then
he did a trick that he'd learned when he was sixteen years
old, what they used to do in Indiana if an old car boiled
over far from a gas station. He unscrewed the radiator
cap, stood on the hood, unbuttoned his trousers, and in

. . . . . . nated a stream three feet straight
. . . . . liator.

As the . . . . . . ed the town, Dillinger and Rojas could see
a huge milling crowd around Ortiz in the main square.

'He's getting them roused up,' Rojas said. 'Why are you
stopping?'

'Too many people.'

'Keep going!' Rojas barked.

'I'll hit somebody,' Dillinger said, the car now going at
a snail's pace.

'Faster,' Rojas said. 'Run the vermin down!'

As Dillinger applied his brakes, the crowd turned as if
it were one person, and everyone, women, children, some
men all came toward the car. These were not a beaten
people, but an aroused mob.

Dillinger could hear Ortiz yelling, 'There in the car is
Rivera's man Rojas, the murderer's murderer, who will
not use dynamite to free our trapped people.'

Rojas knew how to read faces.

'Back this out of here,' Rojas ordered.

'You drive it,' Dillinger said, putting on the hand brake
and getting out of the car.

'I don't know how to drive, you idiot!' Rojas yelled.
'Get back in here.'

'Put the gun down in the driver's seat. Gently.'

Rojas was livid, but when he turned to face the mob,
he knew that however many he might shoot, before he
could reload they would be at him like ants, choking him,
stomping on him, then stringing him up. Carefully, he put
the gun down in the driver's seat. Dillinger picked up the
gun as he slid behind the wheel and slowly backed the car
away from the mob, then turned, and sped out of town,
holding the wheel with his left hand, the gun aimed at
Rojas in his right, and at the top of his voice singing the

song that was on the Hit Parade when he left home, 'Who's Afraid of the Big Bad Wolf?'

Ortiz rode hard for almost half an hour before reaching an encampment of five wickiups grouped beside a small pool of water in a horseshoe of rock that sheltered them from the wind.

The carcass of a small deer roasted over a fire on an improvised spit and three young Indians squatted beside it smoking cigarettes.

He dismounted and tethered his pony and gazed at them impassively for a moment, then went into his wickiup, lay on his face and closed his eyes.

In the darkness there was only a deep satisfaction and a hate that burned like a white-hot flame, so pure that it was an ecstasy, a mystical reality as great as any the fathers at Nacozari had told him about.

Ortiz decided what he must do. He left the peace of the wickiup and assembled his warriors.

He said, 'I have worn a priest's cassock in the hope that I would one day be received as a man of God. Today, I saw Father Tomas, a man of God, shot in the head by that butcher Rivera. Before everything, I am an Apache,' he said, and with one rent of his powerful hands ripped the cassock from his body and flung it aside. Underneath he was wearing the breech-clout and on his head he now put the headband of an Apache warrior.

He continued, 'This is what we must do. Chato and Cochin, go for those of our brothers who would join us in this thing. Ride to the north pasture, break down the fences and slaughter some of the cattle. You will not harm the herdsman. He must be spared to carry the news to Rivera.'

He turned to the third man. 'You, Kata, get as many rifles as we have hidden and come back here to me.'

They moved to do his bidding and within a few minutes

115

he was alone listening to the sound of them vanishing into the dusk.

He stood for a while, thinking, then picked up a handful of dust and tossed it into the fire. In his veins, he felt the fire of vengeance.

IO

As he drove, Dillinger was lecturing Rojas. 'When I was a kid,' he said, 'I learned that some people have big fists and small brains. Other guys have lots of brains but their fists are useless. And some have brains and fists and know how to use them both. I've been trying to pigeonhole you, Rojas, and I figure you for the first kind, big fists, small brains.'

'*Gringo*, I will get you to the Federalistas, sooner or later, just as Senor Rivera wants.'

Dillinger applied his right foot to the brakes so hard Rojas went flying into the windshield, hurting his nose and forehead. 'Sorry', Dillinger said. 'I thought I saw a snake in the road.'

'You drive this car like a crazy madman.'

'Then I guess you'd better just get out,' Dillinger said, waving Rojas's gun at him. 'Out!'

'You can't make me get out here. Take me to the hacienda.'

'I can take you back to town, how about that?'

'No.'

'Well, that's where I'm going, Rojas. Out!'

'Suppose no one comes by?' Rojas, said, getting out of the convertible.

'Somone'll come by. If it ain't people, it'll be your own kind, vultures, coyotes, somebody,' Dillinger said, laughing, as he swung the car around, sending up a cloud of dust to envelop Rojas.

A couple of miles towards town Dillinger spotted some desert wild flowers growing out of an outcropping of rock not too far from the road. He stopped the Chevvy and picked an even dozen of the flowers, put them carefully on the back seat.

The town seemed deserted.

Inside the hotel saloon, Chavasse greeted him with a wave.

'Rose upstairs?'

Chavasse nodded. Dillinger didn't see any reaction of jealousy in Chavasse's face. Wouldn't he have been if . . .?

Upstairs, he knocked on her door, keeping the bunch of wild flowers behind his back.

'Who is it?' her voice said. Amazing how just her voice could get him going.

'Your favourite outlaw,' he said, touching his moustache with his free hand.

She opened the door, wearing a dark green kimono with silver and gold bands around the sleeves. With one hand she clasped the front of the kimono closed, but the top of one breast showed just a smidgin. It was enough. He remembered when the girl before Billie Frechette would sometimes greet him at the door with nothing on top. This woman was different. His feeling was different.

'I thought you were being turned over to the authorities?' she said.

'You sound like an authority to me. Can I come in?' he whipped the flowers around, startling her.

'Oh, they're beautiful,' she said, turning to find something to put them in. She used a pitcher as a vase. 'Your face looks better from your fight with Rojas,' she said.

'Your face looks better to me all the time, too,' he said.

And then he puts his arms around her. 'You'd better close the door,' he said. 'It's all right. I'm on good behaviour.' But his heart was beating like a tight drum.

Fallon, waking, gave a long, shuddering sigh, rubbed his knuckles into his bloodshot eyes and pushed himself up. After a while he swung his legs to the floor and padded across to the window. In the grey light of dawn the mountains seemed forbidding, and in the village great balls of tumbleweed crawled along unpaved road, pushed by the wind.

He shivered, aware of the coldness, of the bad taste in his mouth. He was getting old, that was the trouble. If you had to hide out in a place like this, at least it could be for doing something worthwhile, like Johnny, instead of the petty junk he'd gotten into trouble for.

They'd stopped work at the mine last night just before midnight because no one had the strength to continue. They should have used dynamite the way Dillinger had said. It would have long been over, one way or t'other. Rivera had sentenced them to death to save his damn gold.

Now the Indians in the mine knew something he didn't know. That was always the case when they whispered among each other.

Fallon pulled on his hat and coat, opened the door and went outside onto the porch. It was still and cold, the only sound the wind whistling through the scrub, and a strange air of desolation hung over everything. It was as if he had stumbled upon some ancient workings long since abandoned. He frowned and went up the slope.

The ore shed was empty. Usually by this time it was filled with Indians crouched together against the wall, waiting for the first shift to start. The steam engine was cold, something that was never supposed to happen. One of the watchman's regular duties was to keep it stoked during the night.

119

He returned to the cabin, led his horse from the shed at the rear and saddled it quickly. The first thing he noticed as he went down into the village was the absolute stillness. No smoke lifted into the sky from early-morning cooking fires and there was a complete absence of life. Not so much as a dog crossed the street as he rode up to the well and dismounted.

He opened the nearest door and peered inside. The room was bare, even the cooking pots had gone and when he touched the hearth it was cold.

He tried the next house and the next, with the same result, and returned to the well slowly. As he stood there beside his horse, a dog howled somewhere out in the desert, the sound of it echoing back from the mountains. Was it a dog? Or was it one of those Indian signals? In that first moment of irrational fear, he scrambled into the saddle and galloped out of the village.

Whatever was wrong had succeeded in frightening every man, woman and child in the place. He pushed his mount hard and half an hour later reached the head of the valley and rode down to the hacienda.

As he went across the courtyard, the door opened and Doña Clara appeared. Her hair was plaited like an Indian woman's. She seemed considerably distressed.

'Senor Fallon, thank God you are here.'

Fallon looked down at her without dismounting. 'Isn't Don Jose here?'

She shook her head. 'I'm quite alone except for Maria, my maid. My husband went up to the north pastures with Rojas while it was still dark. His herdsman brought the news that some of the cattle had been slaughtered.'

'What about the servants?'

'Usually the cook brings me coffee in bed at six. When she didn't come I decided to look for her.' She shook her head in bewilderment. 'The kitchen is cold, there is no one there. It is like a house of the dead.'

'It may be something to do with what happened yesterday at the mine,' Fallon told her. 'I'll ride down to the servants' quarters. There must be somebody who can tell us what's going on.'

He galloped round to the rear of the house and down the slope towards the cluster of adobe huts beside the stream. When he kicked open the first door and went inside it was the same story. The servants had taken their belongings with them.

As he scrambled into the saddle again, someone screamed up at the hacienda and he dug his heels into the horse's flanks and urged it up the slope. When he entered the courtyard a buckboard was standing at the front door. Doña Clara leaned with her face to the wall, and Felipe, Rivera's vaquero, stood on the steps, hat in hands.

Fallon dismounted. 'What is it?'

Felipe came down the steps slowly, his face very pale. 'See for yourself, senor.'

In the back of the buckboard behind the rear seat lay something covered with a brightly coloured Indian blanket. Fallon moved forward and drew in his breath sharply. Father Tomas gazed up at the sky, his faded blue eyes retracted only slightly. The mortal head wound had turned his face into a grotesque mask.

Fallon covered it with the blanket. 'Where did you find him?'

'No more than a hundred yards from my hut, senor. The strange thing was that the horses had been hobbled.'

'They didn't bury him. They sent the body here as a message.'

Doña Clara turned from the wall. Her face was drawn and very white, but she had obviously regained control of herself. 'Senor Fallon, tell me the truth. What does this mean?'

'What has Don Jose told you?'

121

'He tells me nothing. Please, I must know what is going on.'

'There was a dispute at the mine. Twenty or so men were trapped by a cave-in. The new American suggested dynamite to move a huge rock that was blocking our rescue work. Don Jose refused and ordered the American turned over to the authorities. Father Tomas pleaded with Don Jose. So – I am sorry, Doña Clara – Don Jose shot Father Tomas as an example.'

'I don't believe you!' she cried.

'There were many witnesses.'

'Is that why the cattle have been slaughtered?'

Fallon shrugged.

'Is that why the people have run off?'

Fallon didn't answer her.

'Senor Fallon,' she said, 'I would like you to escort us into Hermosa.'

'Don't you think we should wait for your husband to return?'

She shook her head. 'No, we'll be safer in town. We can go in the buckboard and take Father Tomas's body with us. Felipe can drive.'

She turned without giving him time to reply and went into the house.

Fallon looked up at the mountains as the early-morning sun slanted across them and shook his head.

'Have you got a gun, Felipe?'

The vaquero shook his head. 'The *patrón* keeps all firearms locked in the armoury in the cellar. He alone has the key, senor. We would need sledgehammers to break down the door.'

Doña Clara emerged from the house, a shawl wrapped around her head and shoulders. Behind her the maid carried little Juanita. The women sat on the rear seat with the child. Fallon climbed back on his horse. They turned through the gate and went up through the trail towards the head of the valley.

The sun moved over the top of the mountains, chasing the blue shadows from the desert, and Felipe cracked the whip over the horses' backs, urging them on.

Already the heat lifted from the land like a heavy mist and Fallon wiped sweat from his face with a sleeve.

They dropped down through a dry arroyo and moved toward the place where the trail from the mine joined the one to Hermosa. Beyond this point it wound its way between great, tapering needles of rock and entered a canyon so deep that the bottom was shaded from the sun and unexpectedly cool.

Through the silence a jay called three times and Fallon glanced up sharply. Or was it a jay? Usually they stayed close to water and there was none here. At that moment there was a spine-chilling cry from behind that re-echoed within the narrow walls of the canyon and two Apaches galloped in from the desert, blocking their retreat.

Felipe threw one terrified glance over his shoulder and curled his whip out over the horses. The canyon widened into a deep, saucer-shaped bowl with sloping sides. If they could get to the other end, they would be in the clear. Felipe whipped the horses again. He made out three specks ahead, and as they closed the distance, the specks were clearly three Apaches on horseback. Felipe tried reining in the confused horses, but now the Apaches in front were close enough so that one could raise his rifle in an almost casual gesture and fire. The shot bruised him and again Felipe tried reining the frightened horses, but a second shot rang out and found its mark. Felipe cried out sharply and went over the side.

As the women screamed, the buckboard slewed, the rear wheels bouncing over a boulder. The terrified horses reared up, snapping the lead traces, then burst through the Apaches as the buckboard turned over, spilling its occupants to the ground.

Fallon reined in as Maria rolled beneath him. He lost his seat and went backwards over the animal's rump, falling heavily to the ground. He rolled over and over, half stunned and landed beneath the wrecked buckboard beside Father Tomas's body.

Doña Clara was running for the narrow entrance to the canyon, clutching Juanita in her arms, tripping over her long skirts, her mouth open in a soundless scream. An Apache in an old blue coat with brass buttons galloped behind her, laughing, holding his rifle by the barrel. He swung it in a circle and Fallon could see it curving toward Doña Clara's head and he could do nothing to stop it as the Apache's rifle splintered bone and Donna Clara pitched forward onto her face. Juanita clutched at her mother's body, screaming, trying to shake her back to life.

Fallon looked about him desperately, but there was no retreat. The sloping sides of the bowl lifted smooth and bare into the sky out of the white sand. Rough hands dragged him from under the buckboard.

The Indians lashed him to the rear of the buckboard, his hands behind him. Maria crawled over to her mistress, weeping, then tried to take Juanita in her arms but the child would not let go of her mother. Felipe leaned against the rock clutching a bloody arm. The Apaches were armed with repeating rifles and two of them had revolvers in their belts. Their faces were painted in vertical stripes of blue and white.

What happened then was like something out of a nightmare. One of the Apaches turned Doña Clara over. She was mercifully dead. He went over to the frightened Maria who was begging him for mercy but, his face impassive, the Apache lifted his rifle and smashed her head again and again. He picked up little Juanita, who was now kicking

124

and screaming, and when Fallon yelled, 'Leave the little girl alone,' he lifted Fallon's chin and spat in his face.

Meanwhile, the others had built a fire from pieces of the buckboard. When it was going well they removed one of the wheels, lashed the screaming Felipe to it in the form of a St Andrew's Cross, and roasted him alive, all because they belonged to Rivera.

As the sun rose, the stench of burning flesh became unbearable. Fallon hung there, waiting for his turn to come and his head dropped forward on his chest.

A thunder of hooves caused him to look up as Ortiz rode into the bowl followed by a dozen warriors. Ortiz dismounted and walked forward, pushing aside those who crowded around him excitedly. Unlike the others he wore no war paint, but Fallon took in the red flannel shirt and headband, the rawhide boots. It was enough.

He tried to moisten dry lips. 'Juan?' he said. 'What is this?'

'No more Juan Ortiz,' the other said. 'You see only Diablo now. You understand me?'

'Diablo?' Fallon croaked.

'That's right,' Ortiz said. 'Now say it again. I want you to know that Juan Ortiz exists no longer.'

'Diablo,' Fallon whispered.

'Good,' Ortiz said and he took out his knife and sliced through the bonds.

Fallon swayed slightly, dazed and stupefied, and they brought a pony and pushed him on to its back. He groped for the halter and Ortiz put a hand on his arm.

'You will tell Rivera I hold his daughter, old man. For that I will let you live, understand?'

Fallon lashed the pony and galloped away.

II

When Dillinger went out on the balcony the sun was just beginning to appear over the rim of the mountains. Rose had let him stay the night, but on the couch in her sitting room. He stood there breathing in the freshness of the morning for a while before going downstairs. He had understood love when he was a boy in Indiana because he had loved his dog. But the feeling he had now was different from the feeling he had had toward the many other women. He was happy, yet his heart hurt with the pain of his happiness.

The bar was empty, but there were sounds of movement from the kitchen. He leaned in the doorway. Rose stood at the stove, dressed for riding.

'Whatever it is, it smells good.'

She smiled over her 'shoulder. 'I'm short on eggs this morning. You'll have to make do with refried beans. There's coffee in the pot.'

He found a cup and helped himself.

'Are you going out to the mine?' she asked.

'If Rojas or Rivera tries to grab me again . . .'

'I saw you had a gun last night.'

'It belonged to Rojas. I'm sure he has another by now. Rose, I want to trust you with something.'

'My uncle says never trust a woman.'

'I trust you. When I was a kid, I landed in reform school. That's a jail for kids. And then I was transferred to a

126

worse place. I put in nine years, do you know how long that can be? I didn't hurt anybody. I didn't steal much. But I swear to you, I am not spending nine years or nine days in anybody's jail any more. Rivera knows who I am.'

'Better than I do?'

'He knows my identity. Which is why if he and I can't live in the same place, I've got to move on.'

'That will be sad for me.'

'Unless you decided to come with me.' It was out of the bag. He watched her eyes, those beautiful, slightly slanted eyes, larger than any he had ever seen.

'This hotel,' Rose said, 'is all I have in the world. If I cannot move the hotel, I cannot move. I am like a prisoner, too.'

Just then Chavasse came in and placed a large stone pitcher on the table. 'I don't know what is happening. There is not one Indian left in the place. I had to milk the cow myself.'

Rose turned. 'What are you talking about?'

'They've all moved out. Only the Mestizos are left and they seem to be frightened out of their wits.'

'What have they got to be frightened about?' Dillinger demanded.

Rose frowned. 'I thought it was strange when Conchita didn't bring me any eggs this morning.'

She put down the pan and went through into the bar. Chavasse and Dillinger followed her. The town seemed strangely still in the early-morning sun. Old Gomez, the crippled railwayman Rivera had imported to work the telegraph, came out of his office and locked the door. He stumped down the street and paused to raise his hat to Rose.

'Where is everyone this morning, Rafael?'

'The good God knows, senorita. I have troubles of my own. The line is down again.'

'Are you sure?'

Gomez nodded. 'At six each morning I get a signal from Chihuahua, just to check that everything's working. Then I reply. It didn't come through this morning.'

'What happens now?' Dillinger asked him. This man must know they're looking for someone driving a white Chevrolet convertible.

Gomez shrugged. 'They give me three days to find the break and repair it. If they don't hear from me by then they send a repair crew from Macozari. That's how it works. In theory. Last time it happened it was ten days before they did anything.'

As he went off down the street, a crowd of thirty or forty Mestizos emerged from the church and came down the street toward them.

The spokesman was a large fat man with a greying beard. He removed his straw sombrero and said to Rose, 'Senorita, in the night the Indians have stolen away with our burros. Why is this?'

'We don't know, Jorge,' she said. 'Perhaps it is something to do with the disaster at the mine. Perhaps they thought that Don Jose would force them to labour for him in place of those who have died.'

Jorge shook his head. 'There is more to this, senorita. We are afraid.'

'But what is there to fear, Jorge?'

As if in answer there was a whooping yell from many throats. A bullet suddenly splintered the post at the side of the door, and before the echo of the shot could reach them, a second one rang out and shattered one of the windows. As Dillinger swung round, mounted Indians came over the ridge on the far side of the town, howling like a wolf pack as they moved down among the houses.

The people scattered, most of them fleeing in panic to their homes. Dillinger pushed Rose through the door of the hotel and Chavasse followed.

As Dillinger slammed and barred the door, Chavasse

128

ran into the kitchen to do the same at the rear. Several Indians thundered along the street and shots crashed into the building as the Frenchman returned.

'They've gone crazy,' Rose said. 'This hasn't happened in fifty years.'

Dillinger peered out of the window, his face blazing with excitement. 'Apaches painted for war. I never thought I'd see anything like that in my life.'

Another bullet shattered glass and thudded into the opposite wall. Dillinger drew his Colt automatic. He scrambled across to Rose who crouched by the window. Her face was very pale and there was blood on her cheek from a splinter of glass. 'Haven't you any weapons in the place at all?' he said.

She seemed slightly dazed and wiped the blood away mechanically. 'There's an old revolver in the top drawer of the dresser in my bedroom.'

He handed her the Colt. 'You know how to use this thing?'

Something clicked in her eyes and she came back to life again. 'Of course I do.'

'OK. Hang on here. I'll be back.'

Dillinger went up the stairs on the run, turned along the corridor and kicked open the door to her room. He found the revolver at once, an old Smith and Wesson .45. It was empty, but there was a box of cartridges. He loaded it quickly, then crossed to the door leading out to the balcony.

As he stepped out, three Apaches rode into the court-yard, one of them carrying a burning brand. Dillinger dropped to one knee, rested the barrel of the Smith and Wesson across the rail and aimed low. The heavy slug lifted the Apache from the saddle as he started to throw the brand towards the stables. His two companions flat-tened across their ponies' necks and rode for cover.

Dillinger went back inside, closed and barred the shutters in all the bedrooms and hurried downstairs. As he dropped to one knee beside Rose, she turned, her face pale. 'Ortiz is leading them. I just saw him ride past. He wasn't wearing his cassock. He was all Apache.' She shivered.

'Your friend Ortiz has become Diablo again.'

He peered over the sill. Most of the Mestizos had managed to reach the temporary safety of their homes and had barred the doors. Three or four lay in the street. An Apache was standing over one of them, his rifle butt ready to smash down. Dillinger shot him in the back.

Flames flickered over the dry woodwork of the stables opposite. An Apache galloped past and tossed a great bundle of burning brushwood onto the porch of the hotel.

'Oh no! Please, not our home.' Rose cried.

Flames ran like lightning across the bare boards, flaring up towards the windows so that Dillinger and Rose had to draw back.

More Apaches rode by, firing wildly. Dillinger pushed Rose down to the floor.

Chavasse crawled forward. 'We can't stay here.'

Flames licked in through the window, cracking the remaining glass and Rose got to her feet. 'We'll be safe on the roof. The rest of the hotel won't burn. The walls are made of stone.'

She led the way upstairs. As they passed along the corridor, there was a thunderous crash from below as the roof of the porch collapsed.

At the end of the corridor a wooden ladder in a storeroom gave access to the flat roof through a trapdoor. Chavasse went first and turned to help the others. There was another burst of firing from the street outside.

When Rose had gone up, Dillinger moved to follow. There was a sudden splintering crash outside in the corridor. As he ran to the door, the wooden shutters to the window opposite burst open and an Apache swung a leg over the sill. Dillinger shot him in the face and the man dropped his rifle, and disappeared backwards, screaming as he fell.

It was an old Winchester carbine and Dillinger picked it up, ran back into the storeroom and scrambled up the ladder. As he came out on the roof, Chavasse pulled the ladder up after him and closed the trap.

The roof was surrounded by a three-foot parapet. Dillinger tossed his revolver to Chavasse and moved across to the side fronting the street. A heavy pall of smoke drifted across the town as the stables and other buildings burned.

The Chevrolet was parked in the alley at the side of the stables opposite. An Indian turned his pony into the alley crowding in against the automobile. As he pulled an axe from his belt and raised it to smash the windshield, Dillinger raised the carbine and shot him out of the saddle. The now riderless pony whirled and galloped away.

The Apaches were now attacking several houses at the same time, directed by Ortiz, conspicuous in his scarlet shirt. Three of his men swung a beam of wood against the door of the general store, which stood next to the stables. Dillinger fired once, picking off the one at the back. The Apache screamed, staggering forward into his companions. They dropped the beam and ran for cover, and Dillinger fired after them. He caught a hurried glimpse of Ortiz pointing toward the roof of the hotel, and ducked behind the parapet.

Rose and Chavasse crawled beside him.

'Ortiz has gone mad,' Rose said. 'He must be stopped.'

Chavasse, who knew the Apache better than anyone, said, 'Only another Indian can stop him now.'

'They will not stay for long,' Rose said. 'In a little while, when the excitement is over, they will realize what they have done and the price that must be paid. They will ride into the sierras as their fathers did before them.'

'I'm not so sure,' Chavasse said, 'Ortiz is like Geronimo back from the grave.'

Someone screamed in the street. The Apaches had succeeded in breaking down the door of a house and one of them was dragging a woman into the street by her hair. Dillinger took careful aim and shot him. He immediately ducked behind the parapet as answering fire thudded into the wall.

Suddenly all the shooting ceased.

In the stillness that followed the only sound was the screaming of the woman lying in the street. When Dillinger peered cautiously over the parapet the Apaches had moved into a group, looking up at the mountains. Dillinger raised his eyes and saw a line of khaki-clad riders come over the ridge and start down the slope in a cloud of dust.

'They look like Mexican cavalry,' Chavasse said.

Dillinger nodded. 'Could be the bunch looking for Villa.' Or a white convertible, he thought.

Ortiz called out sharply. Those of his men who were on foot mounted and the whole troop galloped along the street into the smoke.

Dillinger opened the trap and let down the ladder.

Consumed by the fierce flames from the burning porch, the front door had fallen from its hinges, and Dillinger kicked the charred remains into the street. As the others moved out to join him, the soldiers came past the church and galloped toward them, Lieutenant Cordonna leading.

He flung up his hand and dismounted. There were twelve troopers with him and Sergeant Bonilla, who had a length of rope looped to his right wrist, the other tied around Juan Villa's neck.

The bandit sat his horse with ease in spite of the fact that his hands were tied in front of him. He grinned at Dillinger. 'We meet again, amigo.'

He flung up his hand and dismounted. There were twelve troopers with him.

132

Cordonna came forward excitedly, his elegant uniform coated with dust. 'What has happened here?'

'During the night every Indian in the place moved away,' Chavasse said. 'Before we had time to find out what it was all about the Apaches hit us.'

'Why should they do this thing?'

'There was a cave-in at the mine yesterday,' Rose told him. 'About twenty Indians lost their lives. This American wanted to use dynamite to try to get them out but Don Jose refused, and when Father Tomas pleaded with him, Rivera shot him. Ortiz has sworn vengeance.'

Cordonna crossed to the store and with his foot turned over the Apache Dillinger had shot from the roof. He looked down at the painted face. 'How many were there?'

Dillinger looked inquiringly at Chavasse and then shrugged. 'A dozen or fifteen, certainly no more. We killed four or them. They cleared off fast when they saw you coming.'

'Then we must teach them that there are laws now,' Cordonna said briskly. 'Water the horses, Sergeant. We move out at once.'

'What about the prisoner?' Bonilla demanded.

'We must leave him.' Cordonna turned to Dillinger and smiled faintly. 'Perhaps this time, senor, you could contrive to make sure that he does not escape?'

He didn't see Dillinger winking at Villa.

Cordonna saluted Rose gallantly. 'The pleasure of seeing you again is marred by the distressing circumstances, Senorita de Rivera. We shall lay them by the heels, never fear.'

Chavasse said, 'They can run a long way. They know every arroyo, every waterhole in these mountains.'

'So do my men,' Cordonna said. 'Half of them are Indians themselves, remember.'

'But not Apache,' Chavasse said.

133

Sergeant Bonilla turned from the water trough and led Cordonna's horse forward.

Cordonna mounted, adjusted his chinstrap and smiled. 'Before dark, my friends, I promise you Juan Ortiz. Either riding a horse or across one.'

Watching him canter away into the smoke, followed by his men, Villa sighed. 'What a pity that in life we do not profit by the experience of others.'

He slid to the ground and held out his bound hands to Dillinger with a smile. 'Would you mind, amigo? There is really no place I would care to run to at the moment and I find this rope most uncomfortable.'

Ignacio Cordonna had held his present rank for only six months and had little prospect of receiving a captain's bars in less than three years. It seemed only reasonable to assume, however, that the destruction of Diablo and his band would bring his promotion significantly nearer. That thought pushed every other consideration from his mind.

Half an hour later leaving Hermosa they topped a rise and saw a bearded scarecrow riding toward them on an Indian pony. When Fallon caught sight of the uniforms he slid to the ground with a hoarse cry and waited for them.

He was still terribly shaken by his ordeal and Cordonna dismounted and held a canteen to his lips. When he had drunk his fill the old man stammered out his story in a few graphic sentences.

Cordonna turned to Bonilla. 'Four in the ambush at the canyon and perhaps twelve or fifteen have joined them from the town.' He grinned. 'Fair odds.'

Cordonna mounted quickly and galloped away, followed by his men. Within a few moments they were only a cloud of dust travelling fast across the desert. Fallon shook his head, climbed back on his pony and rode off toward Hermosa.

At the entrance to the canyon Cordonna halted and sent Bonilla and a trooper forward. The two men rode through into the great bowl and reined in their horses sharply at the scene which met their eyes.

The fire still smouldered, the heat of it making things lose definition, and the charred body of Felipe, with its unrecognizable face, sprawled across the embers.

Bonilla rode on through to the other side where a broad trail of pony tracks turned into the desert. He dismounted for a moment to examine them and then rode back to his companion.

'Tell the lieutenant to come on in. They've cleared off.'

He dismounted and lit a cigarette while he waited, gazing up at the steeply sloping sides of the bowl, at the rocks above, imagining the poor devils trapped in here with no hope of retreat.

He shuddered and turned to meet Cordonna as he rode in with the rest of the men. The young officer dismounted and walked forward. He examined the bodies, Doña Clara's, Maria's, Felipe's and Father Tomas's, then turned his face expressionless.

'One grave for all of them, then let's get out of here. We must keep after them now they're on the run.'

As part of his equipment, each trooper carried a small military trenching shovel. The men unstrapped them from behind their saddles, stacked their carbines and got to work.

Cordonna and Bonilla stood watching them without speaking. When the wide grave was about three feet deep the lieutenant nodded and they carried the four bodies across and laid them side by side. The men turned expectantly, grouping round the grave, and Cordonna removed his cap and started to pray.

From the rocks above, Ortiz brought the sights of his rifle to bear on the base of the lieutenant's skull and squeezed the trigger. It was the signal to begin. As Cor-

135

donna pitched forward into the grave, the Apaches fired at each of the men below.

Within a few moments it was all over. Here and there an unfortunate trooper still moved or tried to shelter behind the bodies of his friends, but there was no escape. The shots continued until no limb moved. Finally, Ortiz held up his hand and scrambled to his feet.

As he stood gazing down at the carnage, one of his men ran between the boulders and tugged at his sleeve excitedly. Ortiz followed him across the hillside to a point where he could look out across the desert. Two riders were galloping along the trail from the direction of the hacienda.

He ran between the boulders, motioning his men to silence, and they crouched in their original positions. Several minutes later Rivera and Rojas rode into the bowl below.

They dismounted quickly and stood, gazing about them, horror on their faces. Suddenly Rivera caught sight of his wife and stumbled into the grave, pulling away the bodies that half covered her. He fell to his knees. Then, like a man demented, he looked everywhere for the body of his child, but could not find it.

Beside Ortiz Kata raised his rifle and turned inquiringly. Ortiz shook his head.

'He is the one we want,' Kata said. 'Then it is over.'

'He must suffer first,' Ortiz said, 'that is why we took the child.'

12

Rojas and a work party of Mestizos brought the bodies back to the hacienda in a large wagon.

For Rose the saddest sight was watching her uncle pulling himself up onto the wagon and looking at the corpses again.

'Has Juanita been found?' Rivera asked frantically.

'No, *patrón*, she is not there,' Rojas replied.

Rivera looked past the bodies of Doña Clara, Maria and Felipe, and fixed on Cordonna as if it was in the troopers that his hopes had lain. But suddenly Rivera was crying, something Rose had never seen in her life, nor imagined he could do. And so, when Rivera jumped off the wagon, Rose, out of the kindness of her heart, put her arm around her uncle's heaving shoulders.

'I am not grieving for the dead,' he said. 'It is for my *carissima*, Juanita.'

'We will get her back,' Rose said.

'Who?' Rivera said. 'The troopers are dead. I can send someone to the next telegraph station and they will send twice as many Federalistas to avenge Cordonna's death, but by that time who knows what that Ortiz will have done to the child.'

'We will get her back now.' It was Dillinger, standing at Rose's side. 'Provided you do not send for the troops.'

Rivera looked at them, Rose and the American, and he could see what had passed between them.

'Rose,' Rivera said, 'in this moment of my greatest sorrow, I must tell you who this man is.'

'I know he is not Harry Jordan. His name is Johnny.'

'He is a wanted man.'

Rose said, 'He is wanted by me.'

'He is wanted by the police in North America. He is a gangster, a robber of banks!'

Dillinger looked at Rose as if to try to read what was going on in her mind.

She said, 'Uncle, I have known for some time what kind of man he is. That he takes money from banks that take money from people may be an act of justice which is against the law. Johnny,' she turned to him, 'have you ever taken a life?'

'No, except in self-defence.'

Rose whirled on Rivera. 'Yet just yesterday, uncle, you took twenty lives that he wanted to save. Who killed the priest? And how many lives have you taken over the years in order to pry gold out of the mountain. If there is a gangster here, it is you!'

Rivera, his eyes like dark steel, looked at her and at Fallon and Dillinger, all stepping back from him as if he was a pariah.

'I want my daughter back,' he said.

Dillinger said, 'Rivera, you are a businessman. I want to make a business proposition to you.'

Slowly, Rivera turned to fix his gaze on the man he had just reviled. 'Yes, Senor Dillinger.'

So, it is senor again, Dillinger thought. Out loud, he said, 'I'll take a small group into the mountains. Fallon, Rojas, Villa, Nachita as a guide. You can come, too, if you want to, but get this straight. I'm in charge.'

'Continue,' said Rivera.

'Rojas has got to obey my orders like everybody else.'

Rojas started to object but was immediately silenced by Rivera.

'Continue,' Rivera said.

'We'll need guns from your storehouse. Including my Thompson sub-machine gun. I'll need gas from your cache for my car, and horses. We'll get done what the stupid cavalry couldn't do.'

'And what is the other side of your proposition?' Rivera asked.

'If I get your kid back alive, I want twenty thousand dollars of your stored gold and safe conduct to a place on the border where I can cross safely back into the United States. Fallon gets another five thousand dollars of your gold and stays with you only until he gets a pre-arranged message from me that I am safely over the border.'

Rivera thought for a moment.

'I warn you,' Dillinger said, 'don't bargain with me about the price.'

'It is agreed. You can trust me, Senor Dillinger.'

'I'm not a fool, Rivera. The kid and Rose come with me to the border. They go back if I cross safely over.'

'What if Rose decides to go with you?'

Dillinger looked at Rose.

'Nachita can come with us. He can bring the kid back.'

'I accept your proposition,' Rivera said, approaching Dillinger, extending his hand.

Dillinger ignored the offered hand. 'Come on, Rojas,' he ordered. 'Let's get the guns.'

The child Juanita sat in the sand and listlessly played with an old doll, pretending not to be frightened by the Apaches sprawled around her. They were as uncomfortable with the Spanish child in their midst as she was with these strangers with painted faces. Behind them the foothills dropped steeply to merge with the desert. To the west, a great canyon sliced into the heart of the mountains.

Ortiz went up the slope above them, a vivid splash of colour as he moved through the brush. He climbed onto a pillar of rock and looked east. In the far distance he looked for the tracer of dust that he was expecting.

Below, away from the others, Chato and Cochin were whispering. Chato said, 'I know how much Ortiz hates Rivera, but now that we have killed Federal troops, it will be like war. We will be killed if we fail, and even if we win for a while, there are thousands of them and they will drive us into the mountains.'

'You speak the truth, brother,' Cochin said. 'I had hoped that with the coming of better times, to go north into New Mexico, to find some kind of work, to send my own son to school. Now all that is fleeing on the wind because of Ortiz's lust for revenge.'

'If we leave, brother,' Chato said, 'we will be deserters.'

'If we stay,' Cochin said, 'I may become an assassin.'

'Of whom?' said Chato in alarm.

Together they turned, because Ortiz had come down from the mountain.

Rose said to Rivera, 'I wanted to see you privately, uncle, to tell you that despite the angers that have crossed us with each other over the years, I am pleased that you are letting my friend try to find Juanita for you.'

'Sometimes a tragedy brings people together,' Rivera said. 'After this is over, do you plan to go north with your friend?'

'Nothing has been decided, uncle.'

'Thank you, my dear, for coming to talk to me after all these bitter years,' Rivera said.

As she turned to go away, Rivera thought, once Juanita is back in my hands, there will be no one for Rose to go north with. Dillinger will be dead and no one will miss him. Not even Rose after a time.

Rivera led Dillinger, Rose, Chavasse, Villa and Fallon to the company office, fifty yards up the street from the hotel.

The sign over the door said 'Hermosa Mining Company'. He unlocked the door. The main room was furnished as an office with a desk and filing cabinets. In one corner was a metal cabinet, which when unlocked by Rivera, revealed an assortment of arms.

Dillinger pointed to an all-steel door toward the back. 'What's that?'

Fallon, who knew damn well what was behind the door, flicked Dillinger a look that said maybe he shouldn't have asked the question.

'Oh,' Rivera said, 'the gold from the mine, after it has been processed, is stored there before being shipped to Chihuahua. There will be enough in there for your fee, and Fallon's, when the time comes.'

The very way he put it made Dillinger uneasy. But he had no time for such thoughts now. On the top shelf of the metal cabinet he found his favourite weapon, the Thompson sub-machine gun. He picked it up, as if shaking hands with an old friend, and loaded it with one of the hundred-round circular magazines.

'Nice to get this back,' he said. 'I can recommend that shotgun if anybody wants something reliable for close-quarters work.'

Chavasse picked it up. 'Just the thing for me, the worst shot in the world.' He also selected a revolver and pushed it into his waistband.

Dillinger felt funny about Rose taking a revolver and an ammunition belt and strapping it around her slim waist. He handed her a rifle. 'Better take this, too. Don't know if we'll get close enough for a handgun.' What he was really hoping was that she would stay as far back as possible. 'I've always had to take care of women,' he said. 'I never thought there'd be one watching out for me.'

At the hotel a couple of Mestizos were using Rose's horses to clear the debris of the burnt-out porch.

141

'Careful,' Rose was saying. 'Don't damage the main part of the building.'

Just then she saw what she had been waiting for, a single rider coming fast. Within seconds, Nachita was pulling up alongside her, his breathless pony stomping and whinnying.

'What did you find out?' she asked.

Dillinger and Fallon both came over to hear, Chavasse and Villa joining them.

'Ortiz is clever. From where he is, he can see you coming at a great distance. The closer you get to his camp, the harder it will be for you to retreat rapidly. It is a natural fortress of stone, high ground that overlooks the path up.'

'Will he harm Juanita?' Rose asked.

'Not until he gets want he wants.'

'And that is . . . ?'

Nachita nodded toward Rojas, who was approaching with his patron.

'Would he harm her after he got what he wanted?' Rose asked.

'To a man like Ortiz, the wife of an enemy is a piece of the enemy. That is why he killed Doña Clara. The child of an enemy is the same. He has not killed her because she is the meat, the goat tied to the stake that makes the mountain lion come within range of his gunshot.'

Dillinger, who had been silent, now spoke. 'I hope to hell you've got a good plan.'

'In my many moons,' Nachita replied, 'I have learned a plan that succeeds is a good one, and a plan that fails is a bad one. This one seems to depend on whether we can trick Ortiz, or whether, as he plans, he can trick us.'

13

They were making last-minute plans to leave Hermosa. Nachita was to be on the lead horse, Villa, who also knew the territory, immediately behind him. Then Rivera and Rojas, Fallon and Chavasse, all of them armed. Rose offered Dillinger one of her horses, a gentle mare, for the ride into the desert.

'I don't care how gentle the goddam horse is,' Dillinger said, 'I can't ride.'

Rose said, 'I can't believe there is something you can't do, Johnny.'

'I never said I was perfect. How about joining me for the ride in the Chevvy.'

For Rose, who had learned to ride when she was very young, sitting a horse was second nature. 'I don't know,' she said.

'The car smells better than a horse,' he said.

'Not to me. I hate the smell of gasoline.'

'Don't you drive?'

'No,' she said.

'You've never driven?' he repeated unbelievingly.

'Never.'

'Then we're even. Come on, I promise not to try to talk you into the back seat, so help me, Hannah.' He held up his right hand as if taking an oath.

Up ahead, she could see that the others were getting restless.

'All right,' she said, tying up her horse and sliding into the passenger side. 'I don't know how far you will get with this up the mountain.'

'Far enough.' He'd checked everything that was check-able on the car to make sure it was in as good running condition as it could be. He'd cleaned the air filter. He'd vented the gas cans in the trunk so there'd be less danger of an explosion. He'd put in a jerry can of spare water, remembering when he hadn't had any. Though he loved to ride with the top down, he prudently raised it because of the heat and because they might be observed from above and he didn't want Ortiz to know how many people were in the automobile.

'Let them get a head start,' Dillinger said. 'We'll catch up easily.'

'Are you afraid?' Rose asked.

'Afraid of what?'

'I guess that answers my question.'

'Sure, I'm afraid of getting bullet holes in this beauty. I haven't seen a body shop since arriving in Mexico.'

'Shouldn't you be more concerned about a bullet in one of those cans you're carrying back there?'

'A bullet hits one of those, and you and I don't have to worry one bit. Would you rather take your horse?'

'I'll stay where I am.'

'Even in this dangerous, gas-carrying heap?'

Rose laughed. 'You have such an expression on your face. What are you thinking? What are you wishing?'

'I wish we were setting out to rob a bank,' he said.

The night sky was clear, and the moon bathed the desert in a hard white light, making it easy for Nachita to follow the tracks Ortiz's band had made in the dust and sand of the valley floor.

They pressed on without a halt, pushing their mounts hard. Just after midnight the trail turned into the foothills

144

of the mountains. Nachita halted them for a rest and Dillinger got out of the Chevrolet and walked across to a slight rise.

The view was spectacular. The desert stretched to the horizon, and its hollows and canyons were dark and forbidding, thrown into relief by the white moonlight which picked out the higher stretches of ground.

'Beautiful, isn't it?' Rose sat on a boulder beside him, taking off her hat and shaking loose a switch of long hair.

'It is now.'

She smiled momentarily and then gazed out over the desert. 'In a way, I feel that you came because of me. Juanita, my uncle, Ortiz, what do any of them mean to you?'

'Ever since Fallon showed me the picture postcard, I've headed here like I was pulled by a magnet. Your worries are my worries, Rose.'

She turned, her face grave. 'You could still turn back.'

He smiled slowly. 'I never go back to anything. An old superstition.'

'You'll go back to the States, won't you?'

'That's different. That's home.'

'Why are they looking for your car? It sounds like they really don't want you at home.'

'Oh, I'm wanted all right,' Dillinger said, laughing. 'By my friends and by my enemies.'

He put a cigarette in his mouth and Chavasse called out softly, 'No lights. That's one thing we can't afford.'

Dillinger put the cigarettes back in his pocket. 'I wonder just how close we are? We must have come better than twenty miles.'

'Nachita thinks they may have sent scouts down to the foothills,' she said. 'From now on progress will be slower. An hour, perhaps two? Who knows?'

Above them, stars swam in the hot night, and he was

aware of the heat like a living thing crowding in. He wiped sweat from his forehead. 'It's too damned hot.'

Fallon moved across to join them and stood looking to the far mountains. In the distance the stars were already being snuffed out as clouds moved across the sky.

'I think we're in for a storm.'

'In these mountains?' Dillinger said in surprise.

Fallon nodded. 'The heat builds up the pressure during the day. It has to give some time.'

'What's the going likely to be from here on in?' Dillinger asked. 'Will the Chevrolet take it?'

'Wagon trains did in the old days,' Fallon told him. 'Mines all over these mountains then, even a ranch or two. Desert again on the other side.'

Dillinger moved back to the Chevrolet and got behind the wheel. 'They'd sure as hell like to know about you at the factory,' he said softly, switched on the motor and took up his position at the rear of the small group.

They ascended into a country of broken hills and narrow twisting waterways long since dry. The slopes on either side of the trail were covered with mesquite and greasewood and, as they climbed higher, a few scattered pines, rooted in the scant soil, thrust their pointed heads into the night.

On one occasion, Dillinger and Rose had to stop and call to the others for assistance to roll a boulder out of the way so that the car could pass. Later, thunder rumbled in the distance, and the sky over the peaks on the far side of the valley was momentarily illuminated by sheet lightning. The air seemed charged with electricity, vibrant and humming with a restless force that threatened to burst loose at any moment like water running over a dam.

For a while Nachita had been on foot, moving slowly, sometimes even feeling for the trail while Chavasse led his pony. By now the sky was overcast and the moon clouded over. As a precaution, Dillinger drove without lights.

146

'I think a horse would be safer,' Rose said.

They came over a ridge through the pines and found themselves on a small plateau surrounded by heavy brush. The old man turned and held up a hand.

'We stay here till morning. No fires, no lights. We are very close.'

They dismounted and Dillinger pulled the Chevrolet under some pines. Rivera was impatient. 'Why can't we move in now and take them by surprise?'

Nachita shook his head. 'They would smell our horses on the night air even before they heard them and we are lower down the mountain. A bad position from which to attack. There would be no surprise. In the dark they would hunt you one by one through the brush.'

'I thought Indians didn't like fighting at night?' Dillinger remarked.

'Someone must have forgotten to tell the Apaches,' Chavasse said grimly, and turned to Rivera. 'There are seventeen of them up there. Long odds for a dark night on a mountainside with a storm brewing. Nachita knows what he is doing. What he says goes as far as I am concerned.'

'And that stands for the rest of us,' Fallon put in,

Rivera turned and faced them. 'So it would seem I am not in command here?'

'You never were,' Dillinger said softly.

For a long moment there was silence as thunder rumbled overhead, the sound of it rolling heavily across the mountains. Rivera abruptly started to unsaddle his horse.

They tethered the horses at the edge of the small plateau. Chavasse and Villa beat among the bushes for snakes. Rose moved to the rear seat of the Chevrolet so she could stretch out. The others grouped around her, chatting, except for Rivera, who sat in lonely isolation on the far side of the clearing, and Rojas, who seemed to prefer the company of the horses.

They talked quietly, their voices a low murmur on the

147

night, occasionally choking back laughter as Chavasse bantered gaily with Fallon. Rose knew that they were deliberately trying to relieve the tension, to make her feel more secure, and she was filled with a sudden rush of tenderness for all of them. And then a match flared in the night in the direction of the horses. Rojas had lit a cigarette.

Chavasse stifled a cry of dismay and rose to his feet, but Dillinger was already halfway across the clearing. He swung back-handed, knocking the cigarette from the Mexican's mouth, sending him off balance into the brush. As Rojas started to get up, Villa pushed him back down and held a knife under his nose.

'One more thing as stupid as that, amigo, and I shall cut your throat.'

He stood up and Rojas got to his feet, glaring at them, a sullen, dangerous animal about to explode. Rivera saw what was happening and took three quick paces forward and struck Rojas heavily across the face. 'Idiot! It is not just us you endanger. You risk the life of the child.'

Rojas turned without a word and stumbled into the brush.

'He will do as he is told from now on, I will see to that,' Rivera said, and returned to his place. At least he could be in command of Rojas, if of no one else.

Nachita moved to the edge of the clearing and stood listening, head turned slightly to one side.

'Any harm done?' Chavasse asked.

Nachita shook his head. 'We are well hidden here. We must post a guard, though.'

Chavasse volunteered to take the first watch. Rose curled up in the rear seat of the Chevrolet. Dillinger made himself as comfortable as he could in the front, and the others bedded down in the brush around the car. It still hadn't rained and as Dillinger closed his eyes, a great rush of tiredness swept over him and he slept.

148

He was awakened by Fallon shortly after 3 a.m. 'Your turn, friend. Better take your poncho. I think we might get rain soon.'

Dillinger checked to see if Rose was OK in the back seat. She looked like a little girl, asleep with her hands under her cheek. He then went to sit on a boulder beside the horses, his rolled-up poncho under him, the Thompson across his knees. There was a dull ache just behind his right eye. He could have used some more sleep.

No more than ten feet away, Rojas sat glaring at him through the darkness. He was no coward and yet he had seen what Ortiz was capable of. He was not here for sentiment, but because the *patrón* had ordered him to come, and now, for the second time, he had been publicly humiliated.

His last shred of loyalty to Rivera had vanished with that smack across the face. An hour earlier he had made his decision. To hell with them. He would ride out, taking the other horse with him. If the others had only the stupid convertible for transportation, they couldn't all fit in. Some would have to go on foot. If the Apaches caught them, his revenge would be complete.

Rojas had waited only for the American to take his turn on guard duty. He got to his feet, pulled out his knife and moved forward quietly.

In the darkness on the other side of the clearing Nachita had been watching him, and now he called out urgently, 'Jordan, watch out!'

Rojas flung himself forward and Dillinger turned, bringing the barrel of the machine gun down across the Mexican's wrist so that he dropped the knife. They came together breast to breast, Rojas exerting all his considerable strength in an effort to wrench the Thompson from Dillinger's grasp. Dillinger hooked a foot behind the Mexican's ankle and they fell together, rolling between the horses into the brush.

Suddenly Rojas released his hold and drew his revolver. As Dillinger pushed him away, the Mexican fired, the bullet ricocheting from the stony ground into the night. As the rest of the party rushed forward in alarm, Rojas ran headlong into the brush.

As Dillinger scrambled to his feet, the others crowded around. 'What happened?' Fallon demanded.

'If it hadn't been for Nachita, Rojas would have put his knife in me.' Dillinger turned to the Indian. 'Does the gunshot mean trouble?'

Nachita nodded. 'They know where we are. We must be ready for them.'

At that moment, a great zigzag of light struck the rocks, followed moments later by the crash of thunder. The deluge of rain came with a sudden great rush, filling the night with freshness.

Rojas kept running in a blind panic, expecting at any moment to hear shots behind him in the brush. It was impossible to see his hand in front of him. He moved forward, half-crouching, holding his left arm high to protect his face from flailing branches.

Suddenly he tripped over something, lost his balance, went over the edge of a small gully, the revolver flying from his hand into the darkness. He would never find it now. He could feel the apron of shale sliding beneath his weight and clawed desperately for a secure hold. As his hand fastened on a tree root and he pulled himself to safety, it started to rain.

He had to get off the mountain, that much was certain. He blundered forward into the darkness through the greasewood and mantinilla, losing his balance, stumbling from one gully into another until he had lost all sense of direction.

When he finally paused for a rest he was hopelessly lost. The rain was still falling heavily, drowning all noise, but

150

behind him loose stones tumbled down the slope. He stood peering into the darkness, his throat dry. As another shower of stones cascaded down, he turned to run.

Someone thudded into his back with stunning force, sending him staggering to his knees. He turned, flailing desperately, feeling hands reach for his throat.

There were hands everywhere, forcing him down against the ground, twisting his arms behind him. He started to scream and something was pushed into his mouth, half choking him, leaving only the rush of the heavy rain and the sound of unfamiliar voices.

Cochin said, 'If we deliver this one to Ortiz, perhaps it will satisfy him. He was the worst against our people in the mine.'

There was a grumbling from the others, then Chato said, 'Only Rivera will satisfy him.'

'Then what are we to do with this one?'

'Glad I brought the Chevvy now?' Dillinger asked, with everyone except Nachita crowded under the raised top of the convertible. 'Like college kids crowded into a phone booth.'

He didn't mind, for to make room for the others, Rose was sitting in his lap.

'Look at Nachita's umbrella,' Fallon said.

The old Indian had pulled two flat pieces of what looked like thatch from his pack and had angled them over his head so that they formed a peak like a roof and sloped down on either side.

'He's got a portable roof,' Dillinger said.

Chavasse chimed in, 'You don't expect Indians to ride around with umbrellas, do you?'

Suddenly all their attempts at humour stopped. The cry of an owl had pierced through the rain.

'That's no owl,' said Fallon.

'Everyone out of the car, quick,' Dillinger said. 'It's too easy a target.'

They scrambled out into the diminishing rain. Nachita was staring to the north. Something seemed to flit between the bushes on the far side of the clearing.

Fallon's instinct was to head for the horses. Crouching, he ran for the greasewood on the far edge of the thicket where the horses were tethered. Damn, he thought, puffing, he was feeling his age in his bones.

The horses moved restlessly, stamping their feet and snorting. Fallon strained his eyes searching the darkness, his rifle at the ready.

A tremendous flash of lightning seemed to split the sky wide open. A crash of thunder made the mountain seem to tremble. Then a second flash of lightning laid bare the hillside. In its brief light Fallon saw an Apache amongst the animals.

He gave a hoarse cry of alarm. The Apache rushed at him, Fallon fired blindly again and again, but the Indian kept coming, his right hand swinging upwards. Fallon was aware of the knife, but it was too late to do anything about it. The point caught him under the chin, penetrating the roof of the mouth, slicing into the brain.

In the next brief moment of illumination, Dillinger saw what was happening, ran to save Fallon but too late. The Apache and Fallon were sprawled over each other in death.

Gradually the thunder moved away across the mountains and the rain stopped. As dawn began to edge away the darkness, Nachita slipped into the brush. When he reappeared, he reported, 'They have gone now.'

It was Villa, on his knees beside Fallon, who pulled out the knife and wiped it on his pants leg. Rose gazed down in horror.

'He wasn't a cautious man,' Rivera said solemnly.

'If it wasn't for you, he'd be a live man,' Dillinger replied.

Rose put her arm around Dillinger's shoulders.

They took a miner's short-handled pick that had been strapped to Fallon's saddle and dug two shallow graves as best they could, covering the thin soil with rocks as a protection against animals.

It wasn't a time to conduct a service. 'There's one American who won't make it home,' Dillinger said to no one in particular.

They moved out.

It was perhaps half an hour later when Dillinger noticed smoke up ahead, rising on the damp air. He stopped the car and got out and Nachita moved cautiously down through the trees and they followed to where a white trace of smoke lifted into the morning from a clearing in the brush.

They found Rojas, or what had been Rojas, suspended by his ankles from a dead thorn tree above a fire.

14

The Indians were all assembled around Ortiz.

'We started out with more than twice as many as they did,' Ortiz said, 'and none of us is a woman. Now they have lost two to our one. The gods are turning in our favour.'

It was Chato who said, 'Killing Rojas was enough. It was wrong to kill the old man.'

'Silence!' Ortiz said. 'Manilot was told by me to turn the horses loose. The old man saw him and would have shot him. Now they are both dead. The next one to be dead must be Rivera.'

'Do we wait for them here?' Kata wanted to know.

Ortiz shook his head. 'First we must confuse them a little.' He turned to a small, swarthy man in a green shirt and leather waistcoast. 'Paco, take my horse and six men. Ride to Adobe Wells, then circle back here. We will take the pack trail through the canyon and across the mountains to the Place of Green Waters. We will wait for you there.'

'How can we be sure that Nachita will follow Paco and not us?' Kata said. 'The old one is cunning.'

'Which is why he will follow the band led by my horse,' Ortiz said.

'Perhaps they also will split into two groups?'

'There are too few of them.' Ortiz shook his head. 'They sleep lightly enough as it is.'

Paco had already selected his men. He mounted Ortiz's

154

pony and rode quickly down towards the desert. Ortiz turned and looked to the east again.

The dust was a little more pronounced and he thought of Rivera, a smile touching his lips. It would not be long now and the pleasure he was beginning to find lay in the contemplation of his enemy's destruction.

He swung on to the back of Paco's pony, nodded to the others and led the way up into the canyon.

By noon the party from Hermosa had moved into a broken wilderness of rock and sand, crisscrossed by dried-up water courses. Despite the lack of wind, hot air rose to meet them like the blast from a furnace door, lifting the sand into dust devils.

The line of riders was strung out along the trail, their faces covered by scarves against the dust, Dillinger for once leading the way. The grisly discovery in the clearing had had a chastening effect on everyone. Even Chavasse, whose high spirits were normally well in evidence, was strangely subdued as he rode, lolling in the saddle, half asleep.

Dillinger couldn't get his mind off Fallon. He'd gotten to like the old guy without ever knowing much about him. He wondered if Fallon had any relatives back in the States. He had to have somebody, a son or a daughter some place, a cousin, a niece or nephew, somebody. Nobody would ever know he had died, or where. Maybe he could be reburied when this was all over, with a proper marker. Shit, what a lousy way to go.

He glanced back at the others. The trail was much better now as it descended and, on impulse, he increased speed and went off after Nachita who scouted in front.

He came over a small rise and went down to a sloping plateau of sand and shale dotted with mesquite and cactus trees. Several hundred yards away a shoulder of the mountain lifted sharply toward the vast, sprawling peaks of the sierras.

On one side a canyon cut through sand-polished stone. On the other the slope was open to the desert, dropping through the tangle of catclaw and brush over shale and tilted slabs of rock to the desert below.

Nachita had dismounted below the shoulder of the mountain. When Dillinger drove up in the white convertible, which now had a film of sand and dirt on it, Nachita was squatting on his haunches beside his pony, examining the ground. Dillinger and Rose both got out of the car.

The barren soil was crisscrossed by tracks. Dillinger dropped to one knee and frowned.

'They have separated,' Nachita said. 'Nine of them have gone through the canyon, the others down to the desert.'

'Why would they split up?'

Nachita shrugged. 'Perhaps they have quarrelled. Some of the young men, remembering what they have done, will already be afraid. Chato and Cochin confided in me. They think Ortiz is mad to go back to the last century, always fighting, always on the run. If Ortiz kills, they can be punished, too.'

Dillinger took out a pack of chewing gum, offered a stick to Nachita, who shook his head. 'Which way has Ortiz gone?' Dillinger asked.

'Into the desert. His pony had led all the way. Its tracks are easy to recognise.'

The others rode up and dismounted. Rivera came forward, beating dust from his coat. 'What has happened?'

'They've split up,' Dillinger told him. 'Ortiz and a party of six have ridden down into the desert. The rest have gone through the canyon. God knows where it leads to.'

'How will we know which party Juanita is with?' Rivera asked.

Nachita said, 'With Ortiz. He is no fool.'

'I've been this way before,' Villa said. 'A long time ago.

156

An old pack trail goes over the mountains. It's hardly used these days. There's a little chapel in the pine trees on top. Santa Maria del Agua Verde, it's called. Our Lady of the Green Water, because of the spring that bubbles up inside. It's the nearest water for forty miles.'

Nachita shook his head. 'There is water not a dozen miles from here where the foothills of the mountains run into the desert. Once there was a small *rancheria* there. Now there are only adobe walls and a well.'

'And that is where Ortiz is going?' Rivera asked.

Nachita nodded, and Chavasse said, 'It makes sense. He's obviously made those who refused to follow him any longer take the tougher trail. Their tongues will be hanging out before they reach Agua Verde.'

Rivera nodded. 'This time he's played right into our hands.'

'It's too easy,' Dillinger said.

'You give Ortiz too much credit,' Rivera said.

Chavasse shook his head. 'I agree. It does sound too easy.' He turned to Nachita. 'Ortiz knows we're following. How can we hope to surprise him?'

The old Apache permitted himself one of his rare smiles. 'There are ways, but we must wait and see. First I shall scout the trail.' He mounted his pony and rode away.

Dillinger got the canteen from the back seat and offered it to Rose. She drank, then he did. As he wiped his mouth with the back of his hand, he noticed that she was looking at him in a different way.

'Johnny,' she said, 'your friend Fallon knew who you really are. Now the only one is Rivera. If your enemy knows, shouldn't a friend know.'

Dillinger looked at her eyes, the feature that had first attracted him to her. Would the truth blow everything up?

'Come on, Rose,' he said matter-of-factly, 'you know who I am.'

'I know you robbed banks up north. I know you are

157

too familiar with guns. The Federalistas are looking for this car, but *who* are you?'

Women always find out, sooner or later. He knew that.

'If Johnny is the first part,' she said, 'is Dillinger the second?'

'You win the big prize.'

'If I had to fall in love with a thief, why not the best?'

'The best are the bankers. They steal from the people every day and get away with it. When I unload them once in a while, all it does is raise their insurance rates a bit. It doesn't stop them from stealing.'

'You are justifying breaking the law because others break the law, too?'

'That's the whole point, Rose, those bastards don't break the law, they steal legally. We break the law taking it away from them. Is your uncle any different from a bank robber?'

'Yes,' she said.

Was she challenging him? 'How?'

'He's worse. To him, killing is a normal part of business, of getting what he wants.'

'Yet you talk to him like there was nothing ever bad between you.'

'Only until Juanita is found.'

'And then?'

'I must see if I have caught a thief.'

It was perhaps half an hour later that he saw the old man galloping toward him and braked to a halt. Nachita pulled up alongside.

'I have found them,' Nachita said. 'Follow me slowly.'

There was a place in the distance where a narrow spine or rock ran out into the desert like a causeway. As they approached, the old man led the way to the shelter of a narrow ravine. Dillinger killed the engine.

Nachita dismounted from his horse and started up the

158

steep slope. Dillinger and Rose followed. It was hard going and the old man pulled him down just before they reached the top.

'Careful, now.'

They stayed in the cover of some dead pines and Dillinger peered over. Several hundred yards away a ridge lifted out of the ground, dipping in toward the mountain.

Nachita said, 'The ruins and the well are on the other side in a hollow.'

'You're sure they are there?'

'There is a sentry posted in the hillside in a mesquite thicket below the first gully. An open attack would be useless.'

Rose said, 'Why attack anyway? Can't we just negotiate whatever it is Ortiz wants for the child?'

Nachita paused before answering. 'It is possible,' he said, 'that I can approach their camp openly. I can cry out to the sentry from cover, say I am Nachita come to pow-wow with Ortiz.'

'What would happen?' Dillinger asked.

'Ortiz would either kill me or pow-wow.'

'We can't take that chance,' Rose said.

'Even if we were to talk,' Nachita said, 'Ortiz is likely to ask for something we cannot give hin.'

'Like what?' Dillinger asked.

'Rivera's life.' Nachita sighed. 'We will wait for the others.'

Dillinger, sitting on the running board of the Chevvy next to Rose, could see them coming for quite some distance. For the moment there was only the heat and the desert. A small green lizard appeared from the bush a few feet away, life in a dead world. He watched it for a while. It disappeared with extraordinary rapidity as the others rode up.

Rivera stood in front of a boulder, his arms crossed.

The others squatted in a semicircle before Nachita and Dillinger, who explained the situation.

'It would seem that we haven't a hope in hell of surprising them,' Chavasse said.

Nachita nodded and rose to his feet. 'We must make them come to us. It is the only way.'

'And how do we do that?' Rivera demanded.

'I will show you.'

They followed him out into the desert toward a ridge with a narrow gully through its centre making a natural entrance. The spine of rock petered out perhaps a hundred yards farther on.

'Two riders must go out into the desert. Once beyond the point they will be seen.'

'And Ortiz will give chase?' Chavasse said.

The old man nodded. 'The rest of the party will be hidden behind the ridge. Once Ortiz and his men follow their quarry through that gully, the rest will be simple.'

'Why two riders?' Dillinger asked.

Nachita shrugged. 'One man alone might look suspicious, but two might indicate that we also have split our party.'

'And my daughter?' Rivera demanded.

'She will undoubtedly be left with a guard. I will work my way across the mountainside on foot and enter the camp from behind while you occupy them here.'

'It's a good plan,' Rivera said slowly.

'It only remains to decide who is to act as decoy,' Villa put in softly. 'An unenviable task.'

Dillinger sighed. 'I think the bait would look a whole lot stronger if I drove out there in the convertible with the top down as if I didn't have a care in the world.'

There was silence, then Nachita said, 'I agree, but there should still be someone with you. If you are alone, it would be suspicious.'

Rose said, 'He is not alone.'

160

Chavasse tried to object. 'I'll go, not Rose.'

'Wrong,' Rose said. 'If we've been observed before this . . .'

'I'm certain we have,' Nachita said.

'Then we should seem the same. I will be the passenger.'

Nachita said, 'Good, it is settled. Give me fifteen minutes, then move out.'

He turned and ran lightly across the broken ground, disappearing into the jumbled mass of boulders that littered the hillside. The rest of the party started to make ready.

Dillinger took the magazine drum out of the Thompson, checked that everything was working then fitted it carefully back into place. Then he took the clip from the butt of the Colt, emptied it and reloaded again with care, as if his life might depend on it. He put the Thompson on the floor to the right of the accelerator, next to Rose's rifle.

Rose leaned over and kissed his cheek. 'For luck,' she said.

'I told you we'd come out of this thing, didn't I?' He grinned. 'Besides, I've been chased before.' He replaced the Colt in its shoulder holster and put the top of the convertible down. Getting behind the wheel, he said, 'Let's go.'

He turned on the ignition and drove away slowly, waving to Chavasse behind a boulder. Rivera and Villa had taken up positions directly opposite.

Far out in the desert the parched earth faded into the sky and the mesquite glowed with a strange incandescence as if at any moment it might burst into flame.

They rounded the point and moved across a wide plain. A high ridge swelled from the ground between them and the ruined *rancheria*. Dillinger glanced casually toward it but no sound disturbed the heavy stillness.

'Now you know what it is like to be a fox,' he told her.

'This could get on my nerves very easily,' Rose said.

161

At that moment they heard baying. Rose turned to see six of them sweep over the hill and plunge down toward them, in full cry.

Dillinger slammed on his brakes, throwing up a cloud of dust, momentarily concealing them, as he turned the Chevvy, backed up, and then turned back the way they had come, straight at the Apaches pursuing them.

As the bone-dry dust boiled beneath the hooves of the Apaches' horses, they suddenly saw their quarry in the white automobile disappear in a cloud of dust and a moment later emerge heading toward them. They reined in the frightened horses, but the car kept coming right at them, and as the Apaches turned their horses' heads to retreat, they were met by Villa and Chavasse and Rivera firing directly at them.

Dillinger stopped the car sideways across the road. Rose took the first shot at their attackers, hitting one of them, whose riderless horse kept wheeling around. Dillinger was afraid to use the Thompson at that distance, so he gunned up the Chevvy and, his foot all the way down on the gas, ran it straight at the nearest of the Apaches, who lost his balance trying to get his horse out of the way of the charging automobile and slid from the saddle, only to have Villa's bullets thud into him as he hit the ground.

It was all over. Miraculously, none of their group had been hurt. Rivera quickly checked out the dead Indians. None of them was Ortiz.

15

There was no sign of the child at the camp. Rivera was furious. Somehow Nachita had made a mistake. They had followed the wrong group.

Dillinger and Rose left the Chevvy at the side of the road down below and climbed up to the camp in the hollow beside the well. Nachita had lit a fire and squatted before it waiting for coffee to boil. He glanced up and Dillinger walked past him to the crumbling adobe walls.

It was strangely quiet, the heat blanketing all sound, and then a small wind moved across the face of the plain, rustling through the mesquite with a sibilant whispering that touched something inside him.

Was the kid dead? Was all of this useless? He remembered his own childhood, full of hope. When he'd enlisted in the navy, his heart was high, but he'd hated the regimentation. He didn't want to be ordered about by anyone. That's when he went AWOL, got sentenced to solitary for ten days, his first imprisonment. Was all life like that, the smashing of good hope? Or was he just too damned tired now to think sensibly?

Rose came toward him, the Cordoban hat dangling from her neck. Instinctively, she put an arm around him, a bandage around his pain. When she spoke there was a strange poignancy in her voice.

'There's nothing quite so sad as the ruins of a house.'

'Hopes and dreams,' Dillinger said. 'Gone.'

He turned, looking out over the desert again, and she moved beside him. Their shoulders touched. She started to tremble.

There were so many things he could have said as he held her close for a moment.

'Let's go and have a cup of coffee,' he said.

The others were sitting round the fire as they approached and Chavasse and Rivera had obviously been having words.

'What's wrong now?' Dillinger demanded.

'All at once, everything's Nachita's fault,' Chavasse said.

'He's supposed to be able to follow a trail, isn't he?' Rivera said.

Dillinger poured coffee into a cup, gave it to Rose and glanced across to Nachita. The old man smiled faintly. 'We followed the right pony, but the wrong man was riding him. A game Ortiz is playing. He knows that I am leading you. That eventually we must meet. He wishes it to be on his terms in a place of his own choosing. And now six of my brothers are dead.'

Dillinger said quietly to Rose, 'We think of our side, their side. I thought we just won. But for Nachita it means the opposite when Apaches die.'

Rose squeezed Dillinger's hand, but Rivera didn't want to hear any of this. He stood over the squatting Nachita, his voiced raised, saying, 'Where has Ortiz taken my daughter?'

Nachita shrugged. 'Perhaps he will cross the desert to the mountain we call the Spine of the Devil. Near its peak there are the ruins of an ancient city. Men lived there long before my people came from the cold country in the north. In the old days it was an Apache stronghold.'

Villa nodded. 'I have heard of this place. Pueblo – or Aztec. They call it the City of the Dead.'

'But to get there Ortiz must stay on the old pack trail across the sierras,' Nachita said. 'The well at Agua Verde

164

is the only water before the desert. If he camps on the trail tonight he should reach there by noon tomorrow.'

'Then what are we sitting here for?' Rivera demanded.

Chavasse helped himself to more coffee. 'It would take us two days to catch up with him now.'

'Not if we go over the mountains.' Nachita pointed to the great peak that towered above them. 'Agua Verde is on the other side. Perhaps twenty miles.'

Dillinger looked up, shading his eyes. 'Can it be done?'

'As a young man, I rode with Geronimo over the same trail to escape from the horse soldiers who chased us across the Rio Grande.'

'A long time ago.'

'It was a great ride.' Nachita turned and looked up at the mountain again. 'There is a place near the peak where we could spend the night. It is even possible that we could reach Agua Verde before Ortiz.'

Dillinger looked at Villa. 'What do you think?'

Villa nodded. 'The well at Agua Verde is inside the chapel. By the time Ortiz and his men arrive they will need water badly.'

'Perhaps even enough to bargain for my child,' Rivera said.

'If we are going we must go now,' Nachita said. 'We have perhaps four hours left until sunset.'

Dillinger nodded. 'There's no way I can get the Chevrolet over there.'

'I show you.' Nachita took a stick and drew in the sand. 'Ortiz comes from the west. We go straight over and cut across his path in front of him, if we are lucky. You, my friend, take your automobile out into the desert to the north, skirting the base of the mountain. The long way round. A hundred miles at least, but in the cool of the night.' He shrugged. 'And your automobile can travel faster than the wind, is it not so?'

'And what if it breaks down out there in the desert?'

165

Rose said. 'The sun in the heat of the day can fry a man's brains. Or a woman's.'

'A horse could break a leg going over the mountain,' Nachita said. 'Or a man. This way, we have two chances of reaching Agua Verde before Ortiz.'

'That settles it,' Dillinger said. 'Anyone want to chaperone Rose and me?'

'I will come, senor,' Villa said. 'I know this country, you don't.'

Dillinger said to the girl, 'Rose? You want to take Villa's horse and go with the others?'

She glanced at her uncle. 'I will come with you.'

'OK, let's get moving.'

He and Villa put the top up on the convertible. Dillinger got behind the wheel and pressed the starter as Villa scrambled into the rear seat. 'Lead my horse,' he shouted to Chavasse.

Dillinger waved. 'See you at Agua Verde,' he yelled and drove down into the vast desert.

Nachita led them up the slope of the mountain without hesitation, zigzagging between the mesquite and cacti. After an hour they went over a ridge and faced a shelving bank of shale and thin soil held together by a few shrubs.

Rivera, who had been bringing up the rear, now joined them, his face lined with fatigue, 'Why have we stopped?'

Nachita had ridden to a point where the ledge turned the corner of the bluff, and now he came back and dismounted. 'From here it will be necessary to blindfold the horses. Use strips from your blankets.'

Nachita went first and they followed at spaced intervals. When the ledge turned the corner Chavasse sucked in his breath. At this point the trail narrowed to a width of perhaps five or six feet. On his right hand there was nothing, only clear air to the valley floor below.

The ledge lifted steeply, following the curve of the wall,

166

and he climbed after Nachita, holding his horse as close to the wall as possible.

And then the ledge narrowed until there hardly seemed room for man and animal together. He pushed forward frantically and came out on a small plateau. Beyond was a bank of shale and he led his mount up and over the edge of a gentle slope thinly scattered with pine trees to where Nachita waited.

Rivera came over the edge after them and the Frenchman leaned against his mount, wiping sweat from his face. 'Something to remember till my dying day.' He turned to Nachita. 'Can we rest here?'

The old man shook his head. 'From now on it is easy and we can ride. There is a good camp site in the forest on the far side of the summit.'

He mounted and they rode after him. The desert was purple and grey, turning black at the edges, and in the desolate light of evening the peaks were touched with fire.

It was cooler at this height, the air pleasant with the scent of pines, and the climb already seemed remote and impossible.

The ultimate ridge lifted to meet the dark arch of the sky where already a single star shone and they went over and a little way down the other side to a clearing in the pine trees. Nachita held up his hand and they dismounted.

Chavasse felt the weariness strike through him. It had been a long day. He carried the saddlebags across to where Nachita was already building a small fire of twigs and pine cones in a deep hollow between three boulders.

Everyone looked worn down to the bone. Rivera gazed into the fire vacantly, lines of fatigue etched into his face.

For the first few miles out into the desert, the going wasn't too bad, a flat, sun-baked plain over which the Chevrolet moved fast. At one stage Dillinger pushed the car up to sixty and Villa tapped his shoulder laughing like a kid.

'This is better than riding, amigo,' he shouted.

Dillinger had to slow down as they came to a flat brown plain that was fissured and broken.

It was like driving your way through a maze, turning from one ancient dried-out water course into another, travelling at no more than ten or fifteen miles an hour. They ran into one dead end after another, frequently having to turn back and try again, progress was painfully slow and darkness was falling before they finally emerged onto salt flats.

The heat and the dust was unbelievable. They stopped beside a clump of organ cactus and Villa gathered a few dry sticks for a small fire and made coffee while Dillinger topped up the Chevvy's tank with gas from the cans in the trunk. Then he checked the radiator and groaned.

'We must have been boiling away more water than I thought.' He got out the jerrycan. 'I was saving this in case the canteen ran dry and we had to drink this.' He poured what was left in the jerrycan into the radiator carefully, not wanting to spill a drop.

He and Villa sat with Rose on the running board and drank coffee as darkness descended. Dillinger said, 'Good to give the old car a chance to rest.'

'Just like horses, eh?' Villa said.

Dillinger patted the side of the Chevrolet. 'If she lets us down, I wouldn't give much for our chances when the sun comes up tomorrow.'

'Death, my friend, comes to all of us. The dice were thrown a long time ago. The result is already known, but then, you know this, I think, Mr Dillinger.'

Dillinger looked at him calmly. 'Rose knows, but how did you find out?'

'I saw your picture in the paper in Durango a couple of months back. I recognized you on the train, in spite of your new moustache. When we spoke, privately. When you let me go.'

'You told nobody?'

'I owed you, my friend, and besides, we are, after all, in the same line of business. Life is a pretty wild poker game.'

Villa tilted his hat and closed his eyes, turning his back so that Dillinger and Rose could lie side by side through the dark night.

It was in the middle of the night that Dillinger awoke because he felt a hand on his shoulder. He was about to leap up, ready to draw or fight, when he realized it was Rose's hand.

'You are a restless sleeper,' she whispered. 'I only wanted to say I love you.'

Dillinger turned over on his back. The sky was full of unexpected stars.

They got a good start early, the Chevvy making time, when there was a sudden loud bang as the left front tyre burst. The Chevrolet slewed wildly and Dillinger fought with the wheel as the car spun around and finally came to a stop.

They sat for a moment in silence. Dillinger said, 'Anybody hurt?'

Villa said, 'I think I just spat out my heart, a saying we have, but never mind.'

'I'm OK,' said Rose.

'Let's inspect the damage.'

The tyre was in shreds, but the worst was the fact that the rear axle was jammed across a sizeable rock.

'Jesus!' Villa said. 'The horse is dead.'

'Not so fast,' Dillinger said, getting down on his hands and knees and inspecting the situation. He glanced up. 'It seems to me that if we raise her off the rock with the jack and give her a good push she should roll clear soon enough.'

169

It was a solution so ludicrously simple that Rose laughed out loud in relief.

Dillinger got the jack from the trunk and positioned it under the part of the axle that was free. Villa started to pump. Gradually the Chevrolet lifted.

'OK,' Dillinger said. 'Let's try.'

It took both of them and Rose all their strength. For a moment, it looked as if it wasn't going to work and then the jack tilted forward and the Chevrolet ran free.

Dillinger had a spare and the changeover took only minutes.

'OK, let's push on.'

Villa said, 'One thing, my friend. I know Rivera of old. Even if we succeed in this matter, he will send me back to prison to face a firing squad.'

'And me?' Dillinger said.

'My observation tells me that it would be unwise to turn your back on him.'

They got back into the car. Dillinger said, 'So why don't you make a break for it while the going's good.'

'Because there is the child to consider. Because I am a man and Rivera is not,' Villa said simply. 'The same for you, I think.'

Dillinger smiled. Knowing Rose was listening to their exchange, he said, 'It's what we think of ourselves that's important.'

He pressed the starter and drove away, singing another of the Hit Parade tunes that reminded him of home, 'Brother, Can You Spare a Dime?'

16

Dillinger waited for Villa beside the Chevrolet, the Thompson ready in his hand. There was the sound of falling stones and the Mexican came down the slope through the brush above him, his clatter waking Rose in the back seat.

'Nobody there,' Villa said. 'We've beaten all of them to this place, amigo.'

'Great,' Dillinger said. 'So what if Ortiz and his band arrive first? Long odds for the two of us.'

'Three of us,' Rose said.

'True, but the only well is inside the chapel,' Villa said. 'He will need water before trying the desert. If we are inside and he is out . . .' He shrugged.

'OK. What about the car?'

Villa glanced about him at the steep walls of the arroyo on either hand. 'We leave her here and go the rest of the way on foot.'

'The hell you say. Look Villa,' Dillinger said, 'those Apaches find this heap they'll burn it or kick it to death. I want this car. I love it.'

Rose had wandered around a bend. 'Hey, car-lover,' she called out. 'Come and see.'

Villa followed Dillinger past the curve to where there was a huge recess between the stones, a shallow natural cave. 'Drive your true love in here,' Rose said. 'If you throw a few branches over it, they'll never see it unless they smell the gasoline first.'

It was, both Villa and Dillinger agreed, a perfect hiding place. Dillinger impulsively kissed Rose on the cheek. 'Leave it to a woman.'

Dillinger drove the car in as far as he safely could, and then the three of them, like kids, threw brush and branches on it till it nearly disappeared from view.

'Let's go,' Dillinger said.

'Our leader leads,' Rose said to Villa.

'I mean it,' Dillinger said. 'We don't want to get caught here, the three of us against a mob of them.'

And so, over the barren mountainside, through brush and shale, they finally came over the rim of an escarpment and, with a rush of feeling, Dillinger saw the chapel.

It stood four-square to the winds, firmly rooted into the ground at the very edge of a small plateau perhaps twenty-five yards wide and bordered by a few scattered pines and a tangled thicket of greasewood and mesquite.

The chapel itself was built of granite with a roof of overlapping stone slabs perhaps twenty feet above the ground. The door was of heavy oak bound with iron and there were two narrow arched windows on either side of it and a row of similar windows under the eaves.

Villa opened the door and stepped inside, and Dillinger followed him. There was a small altar with a wooden cross, a lantern hanging from a chain, and two benches against the rear wall. It was very quiet, the pale dawn light slanting down from the upper windows. Villa took off his hat and crossed himself as he went toward the altar.

The well was sunk into the centre of the floor and was constructed of some strange, translucent stone shot with green fire that tinted the water, giving the place its name.

Dillinger turned slowly, examining everything. There was a stout locking bar on a swing pin behind the door, and the lower windows had wooden shutters that fastened on the inside.

'Anyone would think the place had been built to stand a siege.'

'In the old days it was a refuge for the mule drivers on many occasions,' Villa said. 'It is a mystery why the water should come up here and nowhere else. That is why they built the chapel in the first place more than two hundred years ago.'

Through the windows on the other side the view was magnificent. The chapel stood on the extreme edge of the shelf looking out across the desert to the Devil's Spine and there was a drop of almost a thousand feet to the valley floor.

'I feel as if I could almost reach out and touch it,' Dillinger said, nodding across at the mountain.

Villa grinned. 'You would need a long arm, amigo. It is at least fifteen miles away. The desert air plays strange tricks.'

They slept the sleep of the dead. When Dillinger finally awoke, he saw Rose still sleeping and imagined what it might be like waking up in a real house in Indiana late on a Sunday morning and seeing Rose in the bed beside him.

There was the slightest breath of wind, a dying fall. But in the sound he detected a footfall. And then another. He reached for his Thompson, got up noiselessly, and then kicked open the chapel door. Nachita was standing in the open doorway, rifle crooked in his arm.

Nachita and Chavasse led their horses in through the door. When all the animals were hobbled together at one end of the building, the old Apache cut a switch of brush from the thicket and walked backwards to the chapel, smoothing their tracks from the sand.

He barred the door and turned to face them. 'When they come, no one must make a move till they have dismounted. Then, with all of you taking aim, I will call out in Apache language. I will go out and bargain with Ortiz while he and his men are in your gunsights.'

'That's crazy,' Rivera said, gesticulating with both fists. 'We should kill as many as possible with the first volley. Then bargain with Ortiz.'

'And kill the child?' said Nachita in anger.

'I didn't say shoot at the child,' Rivera shouted.

'It could be hit by accident. Or any one of them we missed could throw the child off the mountain,' Nachita said. 'I am here to set free a child who is paying for your sins. I am not here idly to kill my fellow Apaches who are following a leader who is as mad as you are.'

Rivera looked ten years older than when Dillinger had first met him. A muscle twitched in Rivera's right cheek. He gripped his rifle tightly. Dillinger was ready to let loose the second Rivera made a wrong move.

Rivera looked at each of their faces. Then to Rose he said, 'What about you? What do you think?'

Calmly, Rose said, 'In all our years, this is the first time uncle, you have asked my opinion as if you meant it. I think all these younger men believe that Nachita, who led us here, should have a chance to do things his way. As he said at the outset, a good plan is one that works. If his fails, there are always the rifles.'

Dillinger had to restrain himself from actually clapping his hands in applause, just as he did in movie houses when an actor said something he agreed with strongly. He'd never thought he'd meet a woman who was more than his equal, and here she was, as brave as a man, and saying the right thing with an eloquence he never had.

Suddenly they all heard the sound of trotting horses.

A moment later the first Apache turned the corner of the bluff and moved into the clearing. Ortiz was almost directly behind him.

He sat his horse with an insolent and casual elegance,

a supremely dangerous figure in his scarlet shirt and headband. The moment he appeared, Rivera gave a sort of strangled cry, and raised his rifle.

'Don't do that, you idiot!' Dillinger shouted.

The shot, badly aimed, caught the pony in the neck and Ortiz pitched forward into the dust. He rolled over twice, came to his feet with incredible agility and plunged into the thicket as Rivera fired again.

His companion was already wheeling his pony to follow him when Chavasse, Dillinger and Villa all fired at once. He toppled from the saddle and his pony galloped back along the trail.

Rivera kept firing into the brush, pumping the lever on his rifle frantically, until Chavasse pulled the weapon from his hands.

'It's too late, you damned fool. Can't you understand?'

Rivera stared at him, his face pale, a translucent film clouding his eyes. Suddenly, eight rifles blasted at once from the thicket, bullets passing in through the windows and thudding into the plaster on the opposite wall.

Chavasse pushed Rivera to the floor and Dillinger and Villa crawled along beneath the windows closing the shutters. In each shutter there was only a small loophole, but plenty of light still slanted down from the upper windows. One or two more bullets chipped the outside wall or splintered a shutter. Then there was silence.

Dillinger peered cautiously through a loophole. Ortiz's pony and the dead Apache still lay in the centre of the clearing. Everything else was still.

He started to turn away and from the next window Chavasse said, 'What's that?'

A branch was being held out into the open, a rag of white clothing dangling from the end and Villa said, 'They want to talk terms.'

'That remains to be seen,' Dillinger said. 'It could be a trap.' He turned to Nachita. 'What do you think?'

175

Nachita shrugged. 'There is only one way to find out.'

He unbarred the door and walked outside. For a moment he held his rifle above his head, then he leaned it against the wall and went forward. Ortiz emerged from a thicket to meet him.

Rivera took a single step forward and Villa swung his rifle toward him. 'I think not, Don Jose.'

For a moment Rivera glared angrily at him, and then something seemed to go out of the man. He turned away, shoulders sagging.

Nachita and Ortiz were talking in Apache, their voices carrying quite clearly in the stillness. There was a sharpness to their exchange. After a while, Nachita turned and came back, leaving Ortiz standing there, shouting things after him.

'What is it?' asked Rose, taking old Nachita's hands in her own.

'Ortiz does not wish to deal with me. He says that because I consort with all of you, I am a traitor to the Apache nation.'

'What does he want?' Dillinger demanded.

'You,' Nachita replied. 'He says you of the white car are the leader.'

'No.' Rose moved forward. 'He can't be trusted now. He might do anything.'

Her concern was plain for everyone to see. Dillinger smiled and put down his sub-machine gun. 'Hell, angel, you take a chance every day of your life.'

Rivera said, 'I am the one who should be discussing terms.'

Dillinger looked at him calmly. 'Thanks to you, I'm not sure we're in shape to do that any more.'

He stepped into the hot sun and walked across the clearing. Ortiz waited for him, hands on hips.

Dillinger halted a few feet away and Ortiz said in

176

English, 'So, you came over the mountain. I had not thought it possible.'

'You haven't asked me out here to exchange pleasantries,' Dillinger said. 'What do you want?'

Ortiz said, 'Take a message to Rivera. Tell him that if he gives himself to me I shall hand over the child. The rest of you can go free.'

'How can we be sure she's still alive?'

'See for yourself.'

He stepped into the thicket and Dillinger followed. They pushed their way through the brush and emerged into a clearing in the pine trees where the ponies were tethered. An Apache squatted beside them, the only one in sight. Juanita de Rivera sat on a blanket a few feet away from him, playing with her doll.

She looked pale, the eyes too large in the rounded childish face, and Dillinger dropped to one knee beside her. 'Hello, Juanita, remember me?'

Her velvet suit was covered with dust, torn and bedraggled. She passed a hand across her eyes and said, 'Will I be seeing Mama soon?'

Dillinger patted her on the shoulder and stood up. 'How much water have you got?'

'Enough,' said Ortiz.

Dillinger shook his head. 'You've come fifty miles at least since your last water hole and you were expecting to find plenty here.'

'Tell Rivera he can have half an hour,' Ortiz said. 'After that there will be no more talking. I have allowed him to live long enough.'

Dillinger pushed his way through the thicket, aware of the unseen eyes on either side and crossed the clearing to the chapel. He stepped inside and closed the door.

Rivera moved forward eagerly, 'What does he want?'

'You!' Dillinger told him bluntly. 'If you hand yourself

177

over within half an hour he'll give us the child and let us go free.'

'You have seen Juanita?' Rose demanded. 'How is she?'

'A little the worse for wear, but otherwise unharmed.' He turned to Rivera. 'What about it?'

The Mexican's face was deathly pale and beaded with sweat. He struggled for words and said in a low voice, 'Is there no other way?'

'From the moment you ruined Nachita's plan for us, we lost any real advantage we might have had.'

'But what about the well? They must need water badly.'

'They could last for a couple of days,' Villa put in.

Dillinger turned to Nachita. 'What would happen if we did turn him over? Would Ortiz keep his word and let us ride out?'

'I'm not sure,' Nachita said. 'He is in this thing too deep. He has nothing left to lose. To a man like Victorio honour was everything. Ortiz is a different breed. Besides, I think he is mad now.'

'What about water?'

'I would say they have none. I noticed the condition of Ortiz's pony when I went to speak with him.'

Dillinger nodded, a slight frown on his face as he considered the situation. He said slowly, 'Do you think he might kill the kid if we turn down the exchange?'

Nachita shook his head. 'If he had intended to kill her lightly he would have done so. I think he will keep her with him now until what happens happens.'

There was a short silence as they all considered his words. It was finally broken by Villa. 'It pains me to admit it, but it would seem that a grand gesture from Don Jose would appease Ortiz only for a moment.'

'I'll test the water one more time,' Dillinger said.

He picked up a canteen, filled it from the well and went back outside. As he crossed the clearing, Ortiz stepped from the thicket.

Dillinger stopped a few feet away. 'Nachita says you have no honour.'

No anger showed on Ortiz's face. He shrugged and said calmly, 'So be it. What happens now is on your own head.'

Dillinger held out the canteen. 'For the child.'

'You would trust a man without honour?' Ortiz said. 'How do you know I will not drink this myself?'

'Only you can prove that you are still a man.'

'Then follow me,' Ortiz commanded.

Once again he led the way into the thicket to where Juanita sat on her blanket. She seemed happy to see Dillinger so soon again. Ortiz knelt and held the canteen for her as she drank. When she finished, the canteen was still more than half full.

'You can have the rest,' Dillinger said.

Ortiz turned the canteen over and spilled the rest of the water to the ground. 'I will drink,' Ortiz said, 'when Rivera is exchanged for the child.'

He handed the canteen back to Dillinger and said, 'Go now! You have fifteen minutes left.'

Dillinger returned to the chapel. The others gathered around him to hear what had happened. He was telling them when he stopped because, he, like they, had heard the muted throbbing of a drum.

'It is their way of trying to frighten you,' Nachita said.

Then came the sound of an Apache chant, voices rising and falling like waves coming in across a beach.

'It is the courage chant,' Nachita said.

'If they attack,' Chavasse said, 'they will drug themselves with mescalin first. They will think they are invulnerable.'

Villa nodded. 'You could empty your gun into one of them and he'll still keep coming.'

'Bullshit,' Dillinger said. 'I've made up my mind. Rivera will be exchanged for the girl.'

179

'No,' Rivera said from the corner. 'I will not do it!'

Nachita stood facing all of them. To Dillinger he said, 'You believe Ortiz because he spilled the rest of the water.'

Dillinger nodded.

'You think he will act with honour?'

'It's a chance worth taking.'

'You Yankees,' Nachita said, 'are naive. You believe what you want to believe.'

Dillinger turned to Villa. 'You bring Rivera out. I'll come with you to take the kid. She's just seen me twice, she'll be less frightened if I pick her up.'

Villa twisted Rivera's arms behind his back and pushed him out of the door.

Outside the chapel Dillinger made himself fully visible so that Ortiz could see he wasn't armed. The chanting stopped. There was a rustling in the thicket across the clearing and Ortiz appeared. Near him, the thicket opened and a young Apache was visible, carrying Juanita in a blanket.

'Put her down!' Dillinger barked.

The young Apache didn't understand him, but Ortiz said something and the Apache put Juanita at Ortiz's feet. It was at that moment that the child recognized Rivera, who was held and being pushed by Villa from behind. She got up to run to her father, but Ortiz grabbed her hand.

'Sit!' he commanded. 'Not yet.'

Then Ortiz advanced to the centre of the clearing. 'At last, Rivera,' he said. Then to Villa, 'I will take him.'

No man in the history of the world could have looked more frightened than Rivera did at that moment, or more pathetic.

Ortiz said, 'Rivera, you died when you shot Father Tomas. You died when you let twenty Apaches die in the mine. Today I merely carry out the sentence.'

Dillinger said, 'Let's cut the palaver. Have the kid brought forward.'

Ortiz motioned to the young Apache, he picked up Juanita in her blanket and again moved her to where Ortiz now stood.

'We will now exchange justice for justice,' Ortiz said, 'life for life.'

'No, you won't,' Rivera said, suddenly lunging for the child, trying to take her up in his arms. Villa, taken by surprise, made a try at holding Rivera back.

In one swift movement Ortiz reached into his clothing and pulled out a long-barrelled Smith and Wesson and, his eyes like a madman's, aimed at Rivera, pulling the trigger again and again. Rivera dropped the wriggling, screaming, frightened child. As Rivera crumpled, Ortiz raised the Smith and Wesson and emptied it at Villa's chest. Then he swooped up the screaming Juanita and ran with her back into the thicket, leaving her blanket behind.

Dillinger could see that the young Apache had been taken completely by surprise at Ortiz's perfidy for he stood like a statute for a second before dashing after Ortiz into the bushes.

Dillinger, betrayed, waited for bullets to thud into him from either direction, the thicket or the chapel. He glanced down at the bodies. Rivera was clearly dead. Villa was still breathing, so Dillinger knelt beside the man, whose breath came in bubbles and whose eyes said it is the luck of the game, and he died.

Chavasse, Rose, Nachita were all coming across the clearing from the chapel, armed with rifles but not firing into the thicket after Ortiz for fear of hitting the child.

Dillinger tried to say something to Rose, but she averted her face.

Nachita said, 'You all go back to the chapel. I will be back soon,' and he went off in the direction in which Ortiz had vanished.

17

They buried Rivera and Villa in a shallow grave in the pine trees. When they had finished, Dillinger returned to the chapel.

He stood at the window and looked out across the desert at the mountain. Strangely enough, he didn't feel tired, but as if he had just awakened from a long sleep.

A small wind blew in through the door, setting the lantern creaking on its chain above the altar, carrying with it the scent of pine, and he could almost hear the stillness.

Chavasse slept peacefully, all strain washed from his face, and Rose lay on a blanket beside the grey ashes of the fire, her head pillowed on one arm. He stood for a long time looking down at her, then filled two canteens at the well, picked up his sub-machine gun and went outside.

Nachita was just emerging from the thicket across the clearing, sweat on his brow.

Dillinger crossed quickly to meet him. 'You are breathing hard,' he said.

'My horse is breathing harder,' Nachita said, 'and he is far younger than I am.' He sat down on a rock.

'Are you angry because I believed Ortiz might be a man?'

'Anger is like rust in the heart. It destroys not the enemy but he who is angry. If I come north to your country, I will trust your judgement about the people. Here, you must trust mine. I bring good news.'

Dillinger offered him one of the canteens. Nachita unscrewed the cap, then drank his fill. 'The news,' he said, 'is that the others have deserted Ortiz. In his dishonour, he dishonoured them.'

'Where have they gone?' Dillinger asked.

'Where has the wind gone? The Federalistas, if they come, will never find them. It doesn't matter. Ortiz is now alone with the child, on his horse, heading into that part of the desert that is near the great rocks in the direction away from Hermosa. He has no reason to keep Juanita now except as a shield from bullets. Where are you going?'

Dillinger checked his Colt in its underarm holster, swung the Thompson over his shoulder by its strap. 'It is my fault he got away. This time he won't.'

'Come back,' Nachita shouted after him. 'You don't know your way about this countryside. Two wrong decisions do not make a right one!'

But it was too late. The American had rushed downhill too fast to hear his words.

Inside the chapel, Nachita knelt beside Rose and shook her gently. Her eyelids fluttered, then opened slowly and she gazed at him. In that brief moment of waking she knew at once that something was wrong.

'What is it?'

'He has gone into the desert.'

Her eyes widened. 'Alone?'

Nachita smiled. 'Men will do foolish things.'

Her nostrils flared, the face becoming hard and full of purpose.

'We'll go after him.'

'Good. We'll take the spare horses. We can move faster if we can change mounts along the way.' He looked down at Chavasse. 'Shall we wake him?'

Chavasse opened his eyes, blinked. 'What is it?'

'Dillinger has gone after Ortiz on his own.'

Chavasse struggled on to one elbow. 'The bloody fool.

183

They'll spread him on an anthill and watch him die by inches.'

Nachita said, 'They do not exist. The young Apaches have abandoned Ortiz because he lost his honour. Ortiz is alone.

'And Juanita?' Chavasse asked, getting up. 'Jesus, we'd best move fast.'

Dillinger threw the brush and branches off the camou-flaged car like a madman. He was sure he could catch up with Ortiz if only he could get going, but it took twenty minutes before the car was clear enough to be backed out of the cavelike crevice carefully, for if it shot back in reverse he'd have gone over the side.

He couldn't wait till he got it back down on the desert so he could pick up speed.

The desert smouldered in the sun, heat rising from the ground to enfold him, and the bushes seemed to shimmer with fire. He wondered how far ahead his quarry was. If he did not know now that he was being followed he soon would. The noise of the convertible's engine echoed back at him from the hills.

He realized how much Ortiz must hate Nachita. The old man possessed the same qualities of strength, courage and intelligence. He could be cruel, that was true, but only in the way that life itself was cruel. He had fought for his nation and seen it defeated. Still, he had retained his honour, and Ortiz had not.

The sun beat down mercilessly, but Dillinger obstinately refused to put the top up. He drove down into a shallow depression and up the other side, pausing to reach for his canteen. He tilted his head, the cool liquid spilling across his face. As he straightened, the desert seemed to move and the mountain to float before him.

There was no sound. Only a great silence. For a moment

184

he was part of it, fused into a single whole. He sat at the wheel as if turned to stone, hardly daring to breathe, and then there was a slight rattle, the faintest of sounds as a lizard passed between two rocks, life in a barren wilderness, the second time such a thing had happened to him. If Rose had been there she would have taken it as an omen.

He didn't realize that Ortiz could observe him. But in fact Ortiz was only six hundred yards from the car, about a hundred and fifty feet higher among the rocks that bordered the desert. He had been giving his horse a rest. The child was asleep on the ground, exhausted. But he had his energy still, and his pride, and now, in his sight, the white convertible, standing still.

Ortiz leaned his left elbow on the rock to steady his arm as he sighted along the top of the rifle. It was too far for accurate fire, but if he hit the car at least, the stupid American would drive closer, close enough perhaps for Ortiz to put a final bullet between his eyes.

Carefully, Ortiz squeezed the trigger.

Dillinger jumped in his seat instinctively when the bullet hit the hood ornament and ricocheted into the right side of the windshield, spidering the glass. In an instant, he turned the ignition, accelerated like a demon, and became a fast-moving target. But no further shots came.

His hatred for Ortiz doubled because of the damage to the car. It was as if the car's virginity had been taken. It would need a new hood ornament. It would need a new windshield. And where in all of Mexico would he find someone who could make it new without asking too many questions? Damn.

Ortiz saw the car moving fast in his direction and kept his finger ready on the trigger. Suddenly, the car disappeared from his view. He frowned, then seeing that the child was still asleep and his horse safely tethered, he moved quickly towards a new position. And sure enough, within minutes, looking between two large rocks, he saw the Chevrolet, not racing as before, but parked, its engine still running, the sound of it now echoing. But of Dillinger there was no sign.

It had been a momentary flash of scarlet from the rocks that had warned Dillinger of Ortiz's new position. He'd parked the car, left the engine running, and got out carrying his Thompson. He figured he'd have to climb two hundred feet to get well above Ortiz, so the hunter could become the hunted.

Rose, Chavasse, and Nachita had been able to make faster time down the mountain than Dillinger, aided by the old Apache's unerring eye for the trail. Once on the plain, they had ridden hard, changing mounts when the horses tired.

It was Rose who spotted the stopped Chevrolet. Nachita had motioned them to slow down, then stop also. It was then that they heard the shot, and even from that distance could see that the car had been hit.

Rose didn't know whether Dillinger had been hit or not, but when that shot rang out, she was certain she loved this man who led an impossible life.

Nachita also decided on the advantage of the higher ground, and so they tethered their horses and started to climb. Soon they reached a flat outcrop and Nachita motioned Chavasse and Rose to lie flat. He crawled forward, then motioned them to crawl forward, too.

He pointed. They saw Ortiz's tethered horse and something very small just waking up. 'Juanita!' Rose's heart sang.

'Careful,' Nachita cautioned, pointing to a position in the rocks almost directly below them. Ortiz was in a

186

sniper's position, waiting. They could not see Dillinger anywhere.

'You and Chavasse go for the child now. When you are almost there, I will get Ortiz.'

Dillinger, recovering his breath, now moved into position where he would be able to see Ortiz. There he was! If he only had a rifle. He had to get closer so that the Thompson would be sure to get Ortiz with the first burst.

He climbed down as quietly as he could. Suddenly, there was a noise off to the right. It was Ortiz's horse whinnying. Rose was clearly visible, running ahead of Chavasse, and in a moment had put down her rifle and scooped up Juanita into her arms.

Ortiz saw this also, and cried out like a madman whose property was being stolen. Dillinger pulled himself up on the rock in front of him, ready to fire his Thompson, but Ortiz, screaming indecipherable words in Apache, was running toward Rose and Juanita. Dillinger saw Chavasse fall to one knee to take better aim at the zig-zagging Apache. The Frenchman fired once, the bullet skimming off a rock, and then a second and third time in quick succession. If he'd hit Ortiz it hadn't slowed the Apache down a second. Dillinger was scampering breathlessly down the rocks, hating the Thompson for the first time in his life because it was too inaccurate to use with Rose and Juanita now just beyond Ortiz in the line of fire.

Why didn't the kneeling Frenchman fire again, Dillinger thought as he moved quickly over the sharp rocks, trying not to trip. Chavasse was looking at his rifle as if it had jammed when Ortiz came close enough to kick the rifle clear out of Chavasse's hands. Out of the corner of his vision, Dillinger saw that Rose had put Juanita down to pick up her rifle. She should never have let go of the kid. She should have run with Juanita in the opposite direction.

Ortiz saw his chance. Instead of stomping on Chavasse

187

as he had planned to do, he ran toward the child, and Dillinger knew the danger. Once the Apache had the kid in his arms, the Thompson would be useless. Dillinger ran as he'd done the hundred-yard dash in high school, at the last moment flinging the Thompson away as he risked everything in one flying tackle, hitting Ortiz just at the back of the knees, crumpling him to the ground.

Ortiz, in his rage, summoned up the energy of a giant, and with a mighty heave rolled over and pinned Dillinger to the ground.

'Get the kid!' Dillinger yelled at Rose, then felt the Apache's fingers tighten on his throat.

Rose, standing ten feet away, rifle in hand, didn't know how to shoot Ortiz without hitting Dillinger.

'Get the kid and run like –' Ortiz's hands, the strongest Dillinger had ever felt, tightened on his windpipe, cutting off his yell to Rose and his air. At least the kid was safe, he thought, but what a way to go.

And then, staring up at Ortiz's face whirling against the sun, Dillinger suddenly felt the handgrip on his throat loosen.

'Scum!' he heard Nachita saying, as he twisted Ortiz's head in an armlock. 'Geronimo wouldn't even have let you hold the horses.'

Dillinger saw Nachita's knife as if in slow motion go in and out of Ortiz twice, and Ortiz's eyes rolled upwards. As Nachita stepped back, Ortiz rolled off Dillinger and sank to the ground.

Somewhere Dillinger could hear Juanita crying. Then Chavasse was standing over him, and then a moment later Rose was kneeling beside him. His breath was coming back, and he knew, like a man redeemed, that everything would be all right.

18

Rose accepted custody of Juanita as if she were her own. As Rivera's closest adult relative, she used her authority to see that Dillinger got the $20,000 in gold that Rivera had promised him. And when Dillinger suggested that Fallon's $5000 go to Chavasse so he could stop being a hotel manager and barkeeper in a strange land, Rose accepted that also. What she could not accept as easily was that, with the passing of weeks, Dillinger had decided to return home.

Nachita accompanied them to the border because he knew a place that was absolutely safe from detection. Rose rode along with Nachita, but for the last few miles she let Nachita lead her horse and she sat with Dillinger in the convertible, both of them aching with their feelings for each other.

'If only I'd met you in Indiana,' Dillinger said.

'If you'd met me in Indiana, you'd have taken no notice of me,' Rose replied.

'I'd have noticed you anywhere,' he said.

When they reached the border, a desolate place with cactus and bramble, Dillinger pulled over, took Rose by her shoulders and said, 'Please come with me.'

'I love you, Johnny,' she said. 'But I cannot go with a man who doesn't know where he is going.'

And so he offered her his white Chevrolet as a gift. 'This way,' he said, 'you'll know I'll come back.'

189

'Because you love the car.'

'Because I love you both. Put Mexican plates on it, have it painted black or red, and nobody'll ever bother you.'

'You forget,' Rose said. 'I can't drive.'

Dillinger looked at Nachita on his horse. He didn't drive either.

And so he said his goodbyes to both of them. 'You know what you need here in Mexico? More banks.'

Without looking back, Dillinger drove across the invisible line that separated Mexico from home. As quickly as he could, he got onto a good road, and then came to a place in New Mexico called Las Cruces, by which time he had decided that he couldn't go on driving a car that the FBI and God knows how many policemen were on the lookout for.

On a side street he spotted a black Ford roadster that looked like a thousand other black Ford roadsters. He parked the white convertible right behind it, and within minutes had wired the Ford to start without a key. Nobody was looking, so he transferred the suitcases containing his gold and the Thompson and some extra clothes and the picture of Rose she had given him that was too big to put in his wallet.

As he drove the Ford away, he looked once in the rear view mirror. That white convertible was one helluva car.

He parked in the business district, and asked a policeman if there was a nearby ice-cream parlour.

'Yes, sir,' the cop said, 'right around the corner.'

Dillinger saluted the cop in thanks.

There were four teenagers at the counter, drinking ice-cream sodas. When the soda jerk came over, Dillinger said, 'I'll have a black and white.'

The chocolate soda with vanilla ice-cream tasted like all of his childhood memories together.

'Ten cents,' said the soda jerk.

'That,' said Dillinger, 'was the best ice-cream soda I've had in a long, long time.'

The soda jerk beamed. 'Those kids,' he said, pointing to the teenagers, 'never say nothing nice about my sodas.'

Dillinger put two bits on the counter. 'Keep the change.'

'Gee, thanks,' the soda jerk said, hoping the stranger would become a steady customer.

But the stranger hit the road like there was no tomorrow, driving through Roswell, Portales, Clovis, and then into Texas, through Amarillo and Phillips and Perryton into Oklahoma, past Hooker and into Kansas, where he pulled up at a gas station in Meade, and used the public phone booth to make the one call he had to make.

The secretary said, 'Mr Hoover, there's a collect call from John Dillinger. Shall I accept?'

J. Edgar Hoover nodded, because you didn't need to put a tracer on a collect call. The operator could tell you where the call was made from. He got on the line and motioned the secretary to pick up the extension so she could write down what was said.

'Mr Hoover,' Dillinger said, 'you can find that white Chevvy convertible, you're looking for in a town called Las Cruces in New Mexico. I don't want you to say I've never been helpful to you.'

Hoover thought Dillinger was very helpful because a line could be drawn from Las Cruces to wherever he was calling from now and they'd know which direction he was headed in.

'Thank you,' Mr Hoover said.

'Don't hang up,' Dillinger said. 'I'm not finished.'

'Goodbye,' Hoover said, thinking you *are* finished.

'Don't hang up, you son-of-a-bitch,' Dillinger yelled. 'I'm the best thing that ever happened to you.'

But the line was dead.

Three months later, on Sunday 22 July, 1934, John Dillinger was shot dead outside the Biograph Movie Theater in Chicago by agents of the Federal Bureau of Investigation. He was betrayed by a woman.